I0726156

It's much
MORE FUN WITH 2
It's much
A MAN'S CONFUSING AND HILARIOUS JOURNEY
THROUGH THE INTERNET DATING GAME
RICHARD ALEXANDER

WORKBOOK PRESS LLC
187 E Warm Springs Rd,
Suite B285, Las Vegas, NV 89119, USA

Website: https://workbookpress.com/
Hotline: 1-888-818-4856
Email: admin@workbookpress.com

Ordering Information:
Quantity sales. Special discounts are available on quantity purchases by corporations, associations, and others.
For details, contact the publisher at the address above.

Library of Congress Control Number:
ISBN-13:   978-1-958176-62-7 (Paperback Version)
                978-1-958176-63-4 (Digital Version)

REV. DATE: 30/03/2022

Its Much More Fun with Two

Richard Alexander

MAN'S CONFUSING AND HILARIOUS JOURNEY THROUGH THE INTERNET DATING GAME

INTRODUCTION

For all men who have enjoyed a long stable relationship and then had to endure the tragedy of bereavement, divorce or separation, this book is for you.

It should cheer you up, provide a great laugh and give you a unique insight into modern woman in preparation for your new life.

Women may also find it enlightening as it gives a valuable insight into male perspectives around dating and relationships.

DEDICATION

TO MY DEAR LATE WIFE LESLEY

Come sail the whispering seas, my love,

Come drift on the tides with me;

For I still long for the wild waves' song

And the silver fish of the sea.

CONTENTS

A SNOWY NIGHT IN SALZBURG

My eyes slowly opened as I tried to focus on the ornate ceiling above my bed and make out all the patterns and the swirls. The weak morning light of a winter's morning filtered through a gap in the curtains. Where the hell was I? And what did I get up to last night?

My head felt rather heavy and my mouth tasted like the bottom of a bird cage so I must have had a good night.

Now I begin to remember, I am in a Salzburg hotel and had a late night on the Guinness, no wonder I feel so bad, its ages since I had so much of the demon brew. Now I must make the effort to close my eyes again and recall everything that happened, hopefully it won't be too embarrassing.

The yellow street lamps reflected the snow and slush on the ground as I made my way through the gentle evening blizzard while dodging puddles and spray from passing cars. I was heading for the Old Town where most of the nightlife was supposed to be. I could see the bridge over the river and the welcoming lights of the Old Town beyond. The streets were almost deserted and the few people around were doubled up and hurrying home to escape the weather.

What on earth was I doing here on this bleak January

day I thought to myself? To be quite honest I didn't really know but had felt the need to escape England for a few days to think through my present and future after recent momentous events.

In the early evening the Old Town was very quiet and I decided to warm up in one of those strange Austrian establishments which are either bars with restaurants or restaurants with bars. I admired the total pine décor, ordered a beer, and sat down beside a roaring fire. As I gazed into the fire, as men have done since time began, my mind began to wander around life's improbables and I began to ponder why, for instance there was only one Monopolies Commission and why there was a Government Minister for women but not one for men.

My mental torpor was disturbed by a movement near the door and a couple in their twenties came in out of the snow and sat at a nearby table. They ordered drinks and then began to caress and stroke each other's hands and fingers with the gentle intimacy of lovers. They gazed into each other's eyes and talked in soft and intimate tones. The girl looked to be in her late twenties with long flowing blonde hair and a short skirt revealing beautiful long legs which appeared to go on for ever. Her flawless pretty face revealed a lovely smile from soft full lips. I could hardly take my eyes off her as I fantasized about having a friend and lover like her and what we could enjoy together.

Sadly, I thought I would never experience anything as good again as I was in my 50's and my wife of many years had died the year before. Tears started to well up in my eyes as I recalled the sadness and the tragedy of it all and the devastating effect it had on our family.

It must have been a couple of minutes before I stopped dreaming and returned to reality only to see the girl staring at me. I looked away feeling very embarrassed, as she probably thought I was a voyeur and not just a normal guy. I gazed back into the fire and let my mind wander again and as an antidote thought about all the women I could have married in my younger and more impulsive days, but thankfully never did.

I finished my beer and got up and left, taking care not to look in the girl's direction again as I was still shy about my behaviour. I suppose if I won the lottery I could have a dozen girls like that but I know they would be there for the money and not the love that I missed so much. Equally had I been a man in my twenties I may have been happy to pursue a pretty girl for sexual conquest alone but in my fifties I knew I needed something more and began to wonder if I would ever find it. Perhaps the real question was how to find it as once you are on your own the entire world seems to consist of couples or maybe its all in the imagination. I decided that the rest of the evening should be devoted to the resolution of this issue over a few beers and plenty of fire gazing while talking to no one.

I stepped out of the door and braced myself in the cold night air then wandered down the main street of the old town sticking to the middle of the road to avoid being impaled by a falling icicle or snowdrift from the gutters of the old buildings four storeys above.

The cold air suddenly made me feel hungry so I decided

to search out a good restaurant which didn't just serve fifty varieties of sausage. The town was still quiet but I came upon a modern looking restaurant called Nordsea which served nothing but fish and seafood from a self-service buffet. I wandered along the long refrigerated counter and looked at what was on offer, some things I recognised and some I did not. I purposefully avoided certain anonymous items which resembled shrivelled willies but was tempted by some large juicy mussels which in my more erotic moments always remind me of women.

I sat at a small table with my selection and the two women on the adjacent table looked over and smiled at me. I smiled back in a rather bashful way and began to realise just how bad and out of practice I was at reading signals from the opposite sex. I had a total inability to differentiate between politeness and interest. In this case I thought I had better err on the side of caution, particularly with the added language differences. The restaurant and food were really nice and I began to wonder why we did not have such restaurants in England, so much more satisfying than burgers and chips.

I walked up to the cobbled square at the far end of the old town and gazed somewhat lethargically at some lovely speciality shops still selling Christmas decorations, much to my surprise. There were beautiful exquisite painted eggs and tree decorations of the highest quality. I hadn't done much for Christmas this year as my wife was always big on Christmas and to try to replicate this would have been too upsetting

As I walked through the square I saw a couple walking towards me, chatting away, looking into each other's eyes, holding hands and swinging their arms. They looked so much in love and tears came into my eyes once again as my head turned to watch them stroll past into the night.

OH GOD, MY BALLS, THAT'S PAINFULL, in my preoccupation with the lovers I had walked into a traffic bollard which resembled an upturned cannon. It was at precisely the right height to give me a severe bruising. Doubled up in agonising pain and trying not to faint I sought a seat on which to recover but there were none so I spent the next ten minutes staggering around the square doubled over doing my Hunchback of Notre Dame impersonation and causing others walking through the square to give me a very wide berth probably thinking I was drunk, insane or both.

Having cooled my sexual desires so comprehensively I decided to call it a night and return to my hotel. I left the old town to cross the bridge and while checking the road for traffic noticed to my right a well known sign for that good old Irish cure all "Guinness". Thinking that this could be the perfect remedy for my present malaise, after all it seems to cure almost everything else if you believe the Irish, I headed for it post haste, or at least with a limp and a purposeful shuffle.

Over the years I had frequently worked in Northern Ireland passing myself off as the genial Englishman abroad, an innocent in Ireland trying to keep out of, and pretending not to understand, sectarian issues. An ignorance of all the folklore and history around King Billy was a definitive advantage in some areas. Equally pretending that the Birmingham four were a pop group had its advantages in keeping you out of trouble in the pubs of Armagh.

Like all Irish pubs the way in was not immediately apparent but after a couple of false dawns I entered a large and rather gloomy cave of a place at around 8.45 pm by my Taiwanese Rolex. Where is everyone I thought as I counted five other customers in a place that would have taken six coach loads of football hooligans?

Anyway I decided to have a nightcap and ordered a Guinness from the barman who was a genuine Irishman by the name of Billy. Its very strange how a quarter of the male population of Ireland seem to be called Billy, perhaps it's in honour of King Billy.

Billy was from Cookstown and we had a good laugh when I told him the last time I went in to a pub in his town my English accent stopped all conversation in the place until they worked out who I was. On the way in my car had also been "clocked" as a strange vehicle by a gentleman in jeans and a bomber jacket leaning against a gable wall to stop an adjacent house from falling down. I gave him a friendly waive to piss him off and let him know that he had been "clocked" too.

Anyway Billy and I had a chat and put the world to rights generally. He casually mentioned in passing that if the place got busy and I needed another drink just to wave at him and he would send one sliding along the length of the bar, but be sure to remember to catch it now.

I thought Billy was being optimistic on a night like this but shortly thereafter the doors burst open and in came a couple of guys carrying an enormous speaker each and proceeded to set them up on a small stage in the corner. Oh good a band I thought, but playing to five people might be a bit challenging. The next crash though the door was the group itself carrying their assorted instruments and within five minutes they were tuning up ready to roll.

I reloaded my Guinness glass courtesy of Billy while the band struck up with their first song which was a promising rendition of the Dire Straits classic "Money for Nothing". I noted with some satisfaction that my Taiwanese Rolex appeared to be keeping good time as it was showing 9.30pm, the same as the pub clock, although unfortunately the date on the calendar was a week out. Nought to worry, for £2.50 it was a bargain and helped to impress the ladies as long as they didn't look too closely.

Within minutes the pub population had risen from six including myself but excluding Billy, to almost three hundred and Billy was rushed off h is f eet w ith t he o ther barmen. He was showing a manual speed and dexterity in dealing out the drinks which would have made Tom Cruise look like a trainee.

Unfortunately, my strategic Guinness position was being encroached upon by the new arrivals who seemed to be mostly university students and staff. However, I decided to test the system and waved at Billy. Lo and behold it worked and I even remembered to catch the fresh glass as it sped down the bar. Those around who w itnessed t he incident were seemingly impressed, probably thought I owned the place or something.

I fell into conversation with an Austrian couple in their late twenties who were delightfully normal and didn't exhibit any tattoos, navel studs or assorted piercings so beloved of English pub populations. It was difficult to chat over the noise of the music and eventually they turned around to watch the group but the girl kept turning back to talk to me from time to time. Given the volume of the music I had to reply almost directly into her ear and she seemed to respond to this with a big and somewhat encouraging smile. As all we men know women have many more erogenous zones than men and I suspect in this case one of hers was her ears. As she was really rather nice I would have loved to have discovered the others!

The place was now heaving and space was at a premium and my friend was being pushed into me by the milling throng. I tried to recall the old maxim that "happiness was a state in which you were no longer plagued by desire" but it just didn't work. The music started up again with renewed vigour and she was bouncing up and down in time to the music rubbing her bottom against my thighs. By this time all the pain in my nether regions had miraculously disappeared and was rapidly giving way to a very pleasurable form of unbridled lust. I thought, am I dreaming this, I am old enough to be her Dad, but I wasn't dreaming and she knew exactly what she was doing behind boyfriends back and the effect it was having on me. Just when I knew I had to have her, or at least her phone number for the next day regardless of the consequences, boyfriend dragged her on to the dance floor.

I waved at Billy for another Guinness to steady my nerves, my slightly trembling hands just managing to catch the pint glass as it toppled off the end of the bar. Just as I thought I had a bit of space around me a group of 5 girls took up position at the end of the bar and ordered drinks. Emboldened by my earlier success I fell into conversation with them. They turned out to be nurses from Kosovo working in Salzburg.

My favourite one who could best be described as "sex on a stick" was mid-twenties, classic features and a lean and toned body to die for. I would have even given her my Rolex if she had asked for it.

However, I was not to be quite so lucky this time as her friend executed a complex manoeuvre which would have drawn admiration from the England football team, which backed me into a corner with no escape. She was a big strong muscular girl in her mid-thirties with a determined manner; I certainly wouldn't have liked a bed bath from her. She was the type who could crack walnuts with her thighs and any man trapped between them would have little chance of escape. Thankfully I didn't notice any tattoos, at least none that were visible.

She was very close to me now and her friends had conveniently drifted off onto the dance floor as if by some pre-arranged signal. I waved at Billy in desperation but he just thought I wanted another drink and slid one down the bar. It was now 1.30am by my trusty Rolex and I had nightmare visions of being spread-eagled across a single bed in the nurse's home impaled upon my new friend while she had her wicked way with me behind locked doors with no means of escape. Her face was now very close to me and I could smell her chewing gum breath on my face. Her ample heaving bosom was even closer and I could feel her erect nipples like rubber thimbles pressing into my chest through the thin material of my silk shirt. Her ample thighs were moving closer and one of her legs was wrapping itself around mine while her face exuded animal lust. She kissed me and stuck her tongue down my throat which was like being attacked by a small but lively python.

My God, I thought, I'm too old for this; I am nearly of an age to retire and should be growing tomatoes or listening to gardener's question time. Would I survive a night with her or would I be just another heart attack statistic in the morning? I have got to escape somehow.

The only way is to go to the toilet where she can't follow, I hope, so I made my excuses, professed undying love and said I would be back in a few minutes. After a decent interval in the loo I had worked out my escape strategy and sneaked out to join the milling crowd of dancers with my legs bent almost double. Many people held my hand and looked on me with sympathy as I danced my way towards the door. They all seemed to think that I was a person of restricted growth enjoying a rare night out. I sashayed my way none too gracefully from dancer to dancer obtaining huge sympathy votes until I finally reached the door and the clear night air. I made my way back to the hotel looking behind from time to time to make sure I was not being followed.

Trudging back through the ice and snow I thought how much women had changed since I last dated some thirty years ago and how so many of the social conventions had been overturned. I was amazed at how forward and predatory many women had become and wondered if the adoption of these and other formerly male characteristics had made women happy. The experiences of the evening had been good for me in a way and wetted my appetite for more adventures.

My eyes slowly opened once again, thankfully having enjoyed a total recall of the evening's events, and I gazed at the ornate ceiling once again

Dammit I thought, Gardeners Question time is so bluddy boring, I am simply not ready for it yet. I will start dating again and this time I will join the modern age and do it on the internet.

AND THAT MY FRIENDS, IS HOW IT ALL BEGAN.

DAISY THE DREAMER

Internet Dating is rather like being in a big sweet shop where there are lots of delicious goods to tempt the palate in a variety of attractive wrappers and you are spoilt for choice. However, until the wrapper is removed and the goods are tasted it is impossible to know if the packaging is better than the reality.

My eyes scanned the pages of individual ladies' profiles, most of them looking for that perfect man to curl up with in front of a roaring fire and share a good bottle of wine. Most of them seemed to have lots of friends but no "special person"with whom to spend happy and fulfilling times and share life's ups and downs. I hoped they would all find happiness but somehow I doubted it as in their fifties both men and women carry considerable "baggage"which complicates new relationships. Existing family commitments, disparities in wealth and health, the aftermath of bereavement and divorce, to name but a few. I forget who said it but there is a wonderful quotation which goes something like this "In your twenties you only see the good points in people, by your fifties you only see the bad", which makes it more difficult to form lasting relationships.

Suddenly I noticed a profile which was a little out of the mould in so far as this lady expressed an interest in Spiritualism and Buddhism, not necessarily in that order. Knowing a little about Buddhism from time spent working in the Far East I decided to make contact and find out more.

Daisy turned out to be a social worker and an expert on counselling which I thought might come in handy if I wished to discuss a problem or two. She sounded reasonably normal during internet conversations but as there is no substitute for meeting I invited her out for lunch.

We met in a pub car park and I waited to greet her as she drew up in her little red car. She was a fairly plain girl with mousy hair wearing no makeup whatsoever, but she had a nice smile and was petite which is the way I like them. Having introduced ourselves I complimented her on the colour of her car and then got the guided tour which was really weird. The rear parcel shelf was crammed full of soft cuddly toys to such an extent it was hard to see out of the rear window. There were pink pigs, fluffy bunnies, teddy bears, miss piggy, cabbage patch and even a small Father Christmas. The passenger side of the front windscreen was festooned with old tickets from assorted parking machines which had never been removed. Draped across the backs of the two front seats was a device which was a seat cover from the front and a kind of multi pocketed holdall from the rear. All sorts of items were stuffed into various pockets including wool, cotton, scissors, post it notes, pens, cardboard, glue bottle and notepads. I jokingly remarked that she could win a Blue Peter Competition without getting out of the car with that lot but I am not sure if she got the joke, because from her point of view, this was normal. Apparently it goes by the name of a "teddy tidy"!

We strolled into the pub, ordered drinks and started to chat. She explained that she went to University in the early seventies at the height of "hippiedom" and this had such a profound impact on her she never really grew out of it. She went on to be a social worker but had never married or had children so unlikely to be too much baggage here I thought.

She was dressed in what could be best be described as modified seventies hippy with

long colourful voluminous skirt almost to her ankles and a white loose fitting blouse. The whole ensemble was held together with various pieces of bright multi-functional ethnic cotton print.

The afternoon passed pleasantly enough and we had an excellent meal, thankfully there were some good vegetarian options on the menu. We talked about all sorts of things but strangely enough she never touched upon the religious side of her interests. Little did I know she was saving this for later.

We met for a drink the following week and continued to get along well together and she invited me to her home that Friday night for drinks and supper.

My mind was racing all week speculating on the possibilities that might unfold for she was really quite sexy below her plain exterior. I double flossed my teeth, had a good shower and applied my weekend under arm spray and a hint of aftershave. Dressed in my best pressed ethnic cotton I strode out to do battle and set off for her place.

As I approached the house I could see it was a large Victorian terrace on the edge of quite a fashionable area close to the university but at the same time not far from the student areas. Clearly she had been reluctant to leave university life completely.

The original front door had been beautifully restored as had the old doorbell which I pressed and could hear chiming within the house. She greeted me at the door and we kissed, I could feel her softness through her thin cotton blouse and a frisson of excitement and sexual anticipation coursed through me. The house was beautifully restored in an extreme Victorian sort of way, fairly minimalist, all stripped pine and brass but delightful all the same. She gave me a glass of wine and I noticed lighted candles were grouped everywhere, she switched off the main lights and beckoned me to sit next to her on the sofa. My level of anticipation that this was going to be a night to remember rose like a barometer and indeed it was; but not quite in the way I had expected, as she had chosen this cosy moment to tell me all about spirituality!

I made myself comfortable and stroked her leg while she explained that we all come from the world of the spirit and our spirit enters us at the time of conception and leaves us at the time of death, going back to the spirit world. Some people known as mediums can communicate with the spirit world and act as a conduit for messages from the dead to loved ones still living. There is no concept of time in the spirit world and even if a spirit has to wait fifty years to see a loved one it will just seem like the next day. The spirit is comforted and wrapped in the arms of God and surrounded by his love and his very being.

Even pets are catered for and apparently many stay with their owners in spirit form and owners are aware of their presence and can talk to them. Others go to the spirit world and enjoy happiness there where the life cycle of reincarnation continues as with humans.

Interesting though this was my mind began to wander when she went on about Jasper, Ernest and Lillie and I was unsure if these were blokes or spirits. As I looked around the room I spotted the bedroom door was slightly ajar and through it I could see a very comfortable double bed and beautiful ornate brass headboard with a substantial footboard as an added bonus. Given a choice of sex or religion on any day of the week I am afraid I would always choose sex.

She seemed to have stopped talking so I looked into her eyes signalling sympathy and great interest and she asked me if I would like to share a spliff. Being just pre marihuana generation I wasn't really into that kind of thing and when she was no doubt trying dope at university I was in the military where such things were totally forbidden.

Anyway I went through the motions but I found it difficult to inhale as having given up smoking years before it really hurt my lungs. The spliff seemed to relax her and make her dreamy and she then suggested we should try some sex. Things are looking up I thought but what she had in mind was not sex as I knew it but something entirely different.

She asked me if I had tried Tantric sex, I said not but that I had read about it which was a lie for I had no idea what she was talking about.

Tantra is a five-thousand-year old spiritual tradition and it offers an approach which makes women feel sexually confident about themselves and is supposed at least in theory to make men multi orgasmic and to satisfy their lovers in soulful ways. That's the theory anyway.

In Tantric sex you respect and appreciate your partner as the other half of yourself and learn to enjoy sexual excitement without tension. Instead of having a brief and localised orgasm Tantra enables you to move sexual energy around the body and then relax into a series of peaks of excitement. There are seven principal energy centres in the body and these are called chakras together with a powerful energy, known as Kundalini energy which lies dormant at the base of the spine.

When I read more about it later I realised I could have enjoyed pelvic bouncing, fire breath orgasm or exploring the intimate geography of a woman that night but sadly I was still at the beginner's stage and therefore it was somewhat less interesting.

We sat opposite each other on cushions on the floor, still fully clothed and gazed into each other's eyes while gently caressing each other's fingers, wrists and forearms. After about five minutes I was getting a little restless and thought we must move on the phase two soon, but phase one lasted half an hour! Unaccustomed to spending so much time sitting cross-legged on the floor I was getting cramp in my nether regions and my kundalini area was beginning to complain too. Daisy then suggested we move on to the next phase which was remaining on the cushions while synchronizing our breathing, maintaining eye contact and leaning forward periodically to touch foreheads with hands in the prayer position after which we had to say a strange word "namastre".

By this stage my legs were completely locked up, my chakras in complete disarray, all sexual anticipation and desire had receded and I was starting to feel rather sleepy.

I explained to Daisy that I wasn't practised in this art and would like to read up on it a bit so I understood it more before we tried it again. I got up off the cushions and staggered around desperately trying to restore my circulation and ease the pain of cramp in my thighs.

We kissed goodnight at her front door and I bounded out into the clear night air safe in the knowledge that Spiritualism and Tantra sex were not for me.

SAMANTHA THE SLUT

I read Samantha's profile while relaxing one evening with a glass of wine and she certainly sounded lovely. Blonde haired and petite with blue eyes, a Christian with an artistic nature, pleasant manner and a good sense of humour, what more could a man ask for?

I fired off a little note that I hoped would attract her attention and sat back to await a reply. Sure enough the next day there was a response in my mail box. It turned out that she was looking for a new man to share her life with; having been divorced for twelve years and she had her own art business and home not too far away from mine.

After a couple more messages to set the scene I arranged to meet her for lunch at a country pub. I always find a lunchtime first meet is highly desirable as opposed to the evening event. With lunchtime either party can escape afterwards if the meeting is a disaster but if it is a success you can enjoy a nice walk and a bit of gentle hand holding together. Also women understandably feel safer in the day time and it is easier to get round that tricky moment when you finish an evening and you have the coffee moment to decide upon.

Samantha turned out to be pretty much as her profile described, a welcoming energetic little package, five foot two in her stocking feet with blonde hair, blue eyes and a nice smile. She had the combination of small shoulders and full breasts which I found particularly attractive together with a warm smile and a promise of delights to come.

After introductions she decided to park her car in a better spot in the pub car park and I guided her in using helicopter guidance hand signals including the one to cut the engine on successful completion. She thought this was very funny and it broke the ice as we entered the lovely old country pub I had chosen for our meeting.

We enjoyed an excellent lunch and I found out that Samantha was big on fish and was a bit of a health freak. She took over thirty different pills and supplements every day and could recite out loud what each one did for you. She also had an herbal remedy for every malady and I deliberately invented a problem with my foot to see how she would handle it. Of course she came up with a remedy off the top of her head involving soaking the feet in an herbal mixture twice a week.

Samantha had this rather disconcerting way of looking at you, she would gaze transfixed at some point just above your forehead. At first I thought she might be checking if I was wearing a toupee or indeed if my syrup and fig had slipped. Perhaps a bird had deposited something in my hair without my knowing? In the end I concluded it was just her and perhaps it was just a way of showing interest or perhaps her way of hiding a slight double chin, who knows.

Samantha's father, now deceased, had been a reasonably successful businessman with excellent financial acumen but unfortunately this attribute was not passed to his daughter who told me tale after tale of financial disasters and sales of shares at the wrong time. In fact, I concluded that she would have lost money on the Magic Roundabout as her financial management was non-existent. I nodded sympathetically and agreed it was really bad luck which encouraged her to tell me more

While she rabbited on I recalled the advice from the wise old sage regarding male response to female problems. It goes roughly like this. Males are task orientated and look at a problem before coming up with solutions. Women on the other hand will relate and discuss a problem with everyone they can find to listen ad infinitum but THEY ARE NOT ASKING FOR A SOLUTION. Unless they actually ask you for a solution it is disastrous to suggest one. I timidly asked a slightly roundabout question along the lines of "do you have someone who gives you financial advice". This seemed to be something of a revelation to her but she took it well as I had asked as question and not suggested a solution. She thought it a good idea to investigate further!

Her confidence in me seemed to grow and she next proceeded to tell me how much money she had in the bank!! I was quite shocked when she came out with this as it was totally unasked for and irrelevant. I explained to her gently that perhaps she should keep this to herself as it may attract the wrong kind of man but she didn't see the point. I went on to say that as I was comfortably off it would not be of concern to me but a man with less money may be attracted to her for her money and not for herself, without her knowing. Finally, the message got through and she became quite thoughtful. I thought to myself how on earth a bright and educated woman could be so utterly naïve but I had much more to learn about the complexities of Samantha.

With our pleasant lunch over we decided to have a walk by the river in the warm summer air, it was really too good a day to return home. As we strolled along holding hands Samantha proceeded to tell me the intimate problems of her womb although I am grateful she waited until after lunch for these revelations. A whole series of gynaecological detail followed most of which I think I understood involving cysts, heavy periods and possible hysterectomies which made me glad to be a man with somewhat simpler and more accessible plumbing arrangements.

Of course we men are so fascinated by such topics that I decided to change the subject and ask about her first husband from whom she had been divorced for many years but with whom she had had a daughter. When she described him I couldn't believe she would have gone for such a man, long haired hippy type with pony tail and tattoos, liking for a regular bit of wacky baccy. Drifting from low paid job to low paid job with weird lifestyle and political ideas. When I asked her how she had met him she told me he used to work for her father and he had penetrated her on their second date when she was still a virgin and, bingo, she was pregnant. When asked how she had allowed this to happen she explained that she was educated at a private convent school and knew nothing about sex, therefore didn't know what he was doing at the time. How naïve can you get?

Anyway they got married as most people were expected to in those days and she went on to have a very unhappy relationship with this waster who knocked her about a bit.

Clearly Samantha seemed to have problems in her choice of men in addition to her finances, quite how big a problem I was to find out later.

After our very pleasant afternoon I had forgotten about Samantha's religious convictions but she later invited me to a social event explaining it was a kind of Christian sing song. The event was about thirty miles away and as we were driving to it we discovered in conversation that we had a couple of mutual friends that we were unaware of. One was in business in the town and the other were a retired couple with whom she had once been neighbours.

When we arrived at the event it was somewhat bigger and more Christian orientated

than I thought it would be and it seemed to centre on a large marquee in the middle of a field. Before we got out of the car I explained to Samantha that my singing was not of the best and I could empty a pub with consummate ease. This did not seem to worry her unduly and she fumbled behind her car seat and produced a tambourine rather like a rabbit out of a hat." There we are, you can play with that if you like." We went into the tent past lots of smiling well-meaning people and took our place for the evening festivities. This seemed to be some new kind of Christian experience involving lots of singing and dancing rather new age and "HAPPY CLAPPY".

After a short introduction and sermon, the music started and everyone launched into song and dance with great gusto and seemingly no inhibitions. People were dancing around all over the place and shaking hands and embracing their fellow man, and woman. I am afraid I felt a little out of place still retaining a bit of good old British reserve in these matters despite recent trends to exhibit openly all your emotions. I also felt like a complete twat bashing away on my tambourine while pretending to sing. My religious principles have never been strong in terms of organised religion and I began to see the funny side of it all while desperately trying not to laugh amidst all these sincere people. Maybe I am too conservative but it was all a bit too American and Billy Graham for me.

Anyway I managed to survive the evening and after tea and sandwiches at the end suggested in a low voice to Samantha that we might just catch last orders at a nearby pub. Off we went and settled down in a quiet corner of a local hostelry while she started to tell me all about her religious beliefs.

Basically she believed that God determined all her actions and encouraged her to mix with like-minded people but how this reconciled with some of her extracurricular activities which I was to discover later, I do not know.

She believed that whatever happened to her in life was Gods will and she could not influence it or change it in any way.

I asked her about some of the other men she had been out with and, as before, her total lack of judgement came to the fore. One guy told her he was a company director but lived in a little hovel of a house where he had lived for six months without unpacking. He clearly had psychiatric problems and his relatives pleaded with her to handle him with kid gloves. He did not possess a decent set of clothes so she went out and bought some for him, Christian yes, misguided possibly.

Another of her men friends was a chap who belonged to the local Hells Angels chapter who had served time in prison for grievous bodily harm but was now apparently rehabilitated. She showed me a picture, he was an ugly brute covered in tattoos with long greasy hair and a spotty nose.

By now I was beginning to have serious doubts about Samantha but I thought I would have at least one more date to see how she was once we passed the kissing and hand holding stage. I therefore invited her to my place for dinner the following weekend.

I made a special effort in a romantic setting with perfumed candles all around as I knew she liked them. She appeared on the doorstep looking lovely and smelling even better, dressed in a light summer outfit with sparkling dangly earrings.

My sexual feelings were aroused with what the night might promise, I had even changed the bed linen in anticipation and put a few smelly bits around the room to make it more inviting.

We settled down to a pleasant drink and a chat before dinner but I made sure to keep the conversation light as I didn't want to spoil the magic atmosphere. We kissed and cuddled instead and I caressed and kissed her ears and the nape of her neck which quickened her breathing. Just when things were getting interesting a strange smell started drifting in from the direction of the kitchen. Oh sod it something's burning so I had to break off and dash out. As it was I was burning with desire too and couldn't wait to get dinner over with and get down to kissing her in all the usual places and a few she may not have thought of too. I thought of her quickening shallow breathing and making her moan with pleasure and beg for more as she reached ecstasy and orgasm time after time.

We reached the coffee stage and all had gone well, she had complimented me on my excellent culinary skills while I was thinking that I would like to show her a few other skills in my box of tricks when she suddenly dropped the bombshell by saying "DID I EVER TELL YOU ABOUT MY LESBIAN RELATIONSHIP?"

Err, err, no I stammered visibly taken aback and reeling from the revelation. My passion began to drain away from me like water through a colander and for once I simply did not know what to say.

Thankfully she filled the silence gap by explaining that a few years ago she had taken a lesbian lover and they had lived together for six months. I asked her light heartedly, if she still played for the other team but she didn't seem to understand. Apparently she met this woman at, yes, the happy clappy event and as they were both committed Christians they got on very well together sufficient to set up home together without telling Samantha's daughter. This and other family problems together with a new woman on the partner's radar caused the split up of the relationship some six months later.

There was certainly more to Samantha than met the eye and over the few weeks I knew her I also found out that she was subject to very violent mood swings. One minute she was all over me and a few days later she was acting like a bunny boiler. It may have had something or everything to do with the natural cycle but I couldn't live like that.

I decided to do some further investigations into Samantha's background and contacted our mutual friends to see what they knew, seeking an honest appraisal, which I certainly got.

I found out that convent educated miss prim had an uncontrollable weakness for lorry drivers and hippy gardeners and had been known to jump into bed with them just two hours after first acquaintance.

Truth is sometimes stranger than fiction!!

MAUREEN THE MECHANIC

At first I thought that Maureen might be the answer to every man's dream, a lady interested in old sports cars and not just looking at them but fixing them too.

Her profile was interesting to say the least as she had never married, had no children and professed an interest in all things mechanical. She did display a photograph, unlike many ladies, but her features could not be recognised as she was positioned at the far end of a vintage car. However, nothing ventured, nothing gained, so I made contact and asked her out.

I picked her up in my car and sure enough she had not been blessed in the looks department with a plain face, dark curly hair and a rather rotund figure. Still beauty is only skin deep as they say and no doubt she would make a pleasant afternoon companion. She was dressed in an almost identical manner to her photograph in a red padded jacket and it was if she was always on her way to or from a car rally. She wore no makeup or other concessions to beauty and her worn fingernails displayed a patina of used engine oil.

We decided on a light lunch followed by a walk along the river so off we went to a nearby pub. I chose an old black and white place with low ceilings plenty of beams and a dingy, half lit, scruffy look which I thought had character and would suit the occasion. I asked Maureen if she would like a drink and she ordered a pint of bitter which surprised me a little. The drinks arrived and we started to chat, although in reality she did most of the talking. She started off by telling me about the latest gas conversion she had done on a Range Rover and halfway through the description she paused, drew a breath, raised her glass and hoovered half a pint of the foaming brew down her throat with barely a blink or a swallow. I sat there absolutely transfixed with this while she continued with her story.

At the end she picked up the glass again and polished off the other half pint with hardly a discernible movement of her Adams apple.

Spellbound by this scene I timidly asked her if she would like another drink to which she readily agreed, same again please. Mindful of the need to slow down her drinking I suggest we ordered some food and looked around desperately for a menu but could find none. Then I noticed it was all chalked up on a blackboard adjacent to the fireplace. We read through the excellent menu with light and rather heavier options and I thought, I know what she is going to choose! Sure enough I was spot on; I'll have beef suet pie with chips and peas she said in a somewhat deep voice which I hadn't really noticed before. Her second pint was delivered and she launched in to a long story about steam engines and traction engines which was another interest of hers. My mind wandered off halfway through the story and I thought, my God, if I wanted something like this I could join my mates in the pub, at least they all pay their round. I was brought back to the present by a sudden silence and I realised she had paused to pour another half pint down her throat so I nodded assent and feigned interest.

The food arrived and hers consisted of one of the biggest individual pies I had ever seen steaming away happily in the middle of the plate and surrounded by an enclosing mountain range of chips. She is never going to eat all that I thought as she poured half a bottle of tomato sauce over the creation and then smothered it in salt. As her glass was empty I half offered her another drink thinking she would refuse but sure enough she accepted with relish. We are never going to have a walk this afternoon I thought, if she has any more beer I will have to prop her up as we are strolling along. She shovelled a large wedge of ketchup covered chips into her mouth and tried to tell me about rebuilding a Jaguar automatic gearbox at the same time which was rather less than successful and left tomato sauce dribbling down her chin. I handed her a tissue helpfully and pretended to have a bad cough to stop me laughing out loud as she looked for all the world like some kind of vampire on a daytime outing. Having rapidly demolished half the chips and made significant inroads into the steaming pie she sat there holding her knife and fork like Desperate Dan and decided to tell me all about her welding skills.

After this I thought, rather mischievously, that I would tell her all about myself to give her the opportunity to see if she could finish her gargantuan meal and get her out of the pub before she emptied her glass. She finished every last chip and almost a bottle of sauce and her glass was looking dangerously low. I'll just pay the bill I said and rushed up to the bar where the barman sorted out the damage while casting admiring glances at my consort. Good grief I thought, he must be desperate or perhaps he is just impressed with her eating and drinking capacity.

I suggested a walk along the river and thought that after

three pints she may wish to go to the toilet but she didn't make any moves in that direction. We walked down the steps to the river along the path by the bank and I hesitantly held her greasy hand in pretend friendship.

We walked along for about a mile past ducks, weirs, lovely old cottages and a myriad of bird species but I guessed this was not her scene and after a while she suggested turning back and asked if there were any toilets nearby. She looked a bit desperate so I took great delight in telling her the nearest ones were back at the pub. She said she didn't think she could last that long and the path was too public to use with lots of dog walkers about. I suddenly remembered a small cave in the riverbank with a plaque by the side of it which explained that it had been a hermits dwelling in the 15th century. From its smell at the moment it appeared that it had been used as a toilet since the 15th Century so I doubted the hermit would want it back. I guided her down the steps in the bank towards it and said I would stand guard on the path. She must have been desperate as she was yanking her trousers down before I had turned my back so I beat a hasty retreat back to the path. She was simply ages and as I waited I tried to calculate how long it would take to drain three pints of beer from an average size woman but gave up. I also speculated on the accuracy of their aim when compared to the more precise equipment of a man and hoped that she had not emptied three pints of beer down the back of her jeans. She then appeared looking slightly sheepish but somewhat more relaxed and we retraced our steps but this time I was careful not to hold her hand.

On nearing the car, she asked me if I would like to go back to her place for a coffee before going home and curious to know how she lived, I agreed. The house looked really nice from the outside, modern, red brick and quite large. We walked down the central path towards the front door and then we paused while Maureen explained the front door was jammed and she always used the back anyway. We went down the side of the house passing a few derelict cars en route which were awaiting restoration according to Maureen and entered a semi derelict conservatory which gave access to the back door. Into the kitchen and what a mess, stuff all over the place, lots of unfinished projects lying around and kitchen cupboard doors hanging off. Does this girl ever finish anything I thought, obviously not?

She searched for the coffee and a couple of mugs and we retired to the slightly less cluttered living room where I was careful to bag the armchair so as not to join Maureen on the small sofa. I asked her about her earlier years and how she had grown up. Apparently she came from quite a well off family and she had a fairly privileged childhood with pony clubs and good schools and a stable home background. All went well until her mother died in her early teens when she lost that feminine influence and came under the wing of her father who was a very successful consulting engineer. She admitted that she then lost a lot of her femininity and became immersed in a man's world developing similar interests and going to shows etc. with her father. Unfortunately, her father had passed away a couple of years earlier leaving her well provided for but rather distressed and rootless but she was in the fortunate position of being able to treat work almost as a hobby.

This of course explained a lot and I began to feel some sympathy for her. I asked her what she wanted in the future and she thought about this for a while and then said "a husband or partner and children" and I think this was in order to replicate the happy family life she had known as a child. Unfortunately, the biological clock was ticking rather loud for Maureen and I guessed she would not have much time to achieve her dream. She then went on in a really candid manner to admit she had difficulty in attracting decent men who she liked and had not had any sex for years.

At this stage I thought I had better change the subject fast so I asked her about her mother on the basis that the pain of loss was more remote than that for her father. She told me about a loving caring woman who was always there for her but sadly was not there to guide her in her teenage formative years.

She asked me if I would like to see the rest of the house and we had a leisurely wander around in the twilight. When we reached her room she sat on the bed as I admired the view from her window, she then reclined on the bed and then sat up and bounced up and down on it. I knew what she wanted but sadly there were not even the slightest stirrings in my loins for her in that way.

I explained I had to get back and thanked her for her company, gave her a kiss on the cheek and escaped into the night. I did feel really sorry for Maureen who beneath that gruff manly exterior was probably quite a soft woman, but sadly she held no attraction for me.

WENDY THE WHINGER

I had just returned from a holiday in Spain and it was Saturday night with nothing on the box but football. I wandered through my e mails and much to my surprise found one from Pat who I had met together with several other people while on holiday. We used to have a drink and a bit of a laugh and a joke at the bar as part of a rather sociable group.

She was telling me that we had a special relationship and definitely a strong affection for each other which I could simply not recall at all. I do however recall that she was married but hubby was not on holiday; however, I didn't fancy her in that sense and certainly did nothing untoward. How puzzling I thought that she could read so much into an innocent social gathering, are men and women doomed forever to mutual incomprehension even if we do need each other.

I began to recall other conversations our little group had such as where do you come from. Most men could place your town in their mind map with reasonable accuracy providing you did not come from Aldeburgh, Leominster or Crook for instance. But women struggled to place even major towns and mention places further afield, such as Vilnius and Vladivostok, which I took great delight in doing, and they hadn't a clue.

On the other hand, men can never remember birthdays, anniversaries or other important things such as what Aunty Flo said during last year's visit.

By this stage I had become a bit of an expert in deciphering what women put on their profiles and interpreting what it really meant, let me give you some examples

No picture means

Ugly or Married and doesn't want hubby to find out or

Lives in a small village and does not wish to be recognised or

If she offers to send you a picture she is probably married.

Are you sure she has given you her correct name and town?

The picture could have been taken ten years ago

If you receive a profile from abroad, do be careful, here is your checklist:

Be very wary if there are lots of glamour photos and little description

Hello I am from Manila/Bangkok and very beautiful and wish to

Marry you, obtain a good passport, and fall out with you two years later

Then divorce you with the help of legal aid and screw you for every penny

If I can't manage the above, I will bring out all my relatives to live with us

I will also nag you to death until you agree to pay for a new well in my grannie's village.

I have several tattoos and a couple of body piercings

She could well be into domination, weird sexual practices, an occasional evening of S&M and a liking for the odd bit of electric lettuce.

Tubby means big

Cuddly means bigger

Home maker – could be looking for a lifetime meal ticket

Animal lover – may love them much more than you!

Fun Loving - could be a total drunk, possibly with a complementary drug habit.

Adventurous - could be into kinky, unconventional or even unsafe sexual practices.

Sensual - likes soft lights, lots of candles, the odd joint and lots of touching and stroking, you just have to be patient.

High Standards/demanding - Impossible to live with and sets ridiculously high standards which only superman can reach and then only with his Y fronts outside his trousers.

Looking for a causal relationship – wants a bit on the side, possibly when hubby is away on an extended business trip.

Loves theatre/restaurants/dancing and walking - helps fill the space when you don't know what else to put.

Of course it is not just women who make mistakes on their profiles, here are some common bloomers which men are guilty of

Poor spelling and grammar creates a bad first impression.

Don't admit you have a nickname such as "big boy" or "sex machine" I know you may be surprised but it's a turn off for most women.

Don't make sexy or rude jokes on the net before you have met her, she may get the impression that you are a relative of Bernard Manning or Jack the Ripper.

Don't put your car on your pictures, women are not interested and may think you are an anorak.

Don't put your house on your pictures, if it's a good one you may attract gold diggers.

Try to give yourself a cultured hobby or interest to show you are a cut above the rest

Don't boast that your personal endowment is the size of a baby's arm, most women will be turned off by this, but see tattoos and piercings above.

When responding to a woman's photograph don't tell her she has breasts like a pair of puppies, instead be more subtle and compliment her by saying she looks pretty or is wearing a lovely dress

If you are in to slightly non mainstream sexual practices such as spanking, don't admit it until at least the third date when hopefully you have gained the woman's confidence, but see Adventurous and fun loving above.

Think up a hobby that women could also relate to, for example horse riding or tennis. Don't even think of ballet or flower arranging, she may think you are gay.

Don't make too much of a fuss about women's dress or clothes generally other than a passing compliment. If you overdo it she may think you are a Trannie.

Try not to tell too many lies, women are inquisitive creatures and you will be rumbled for sure.

Don't let e mail correspondence drag on for too long, ask her out. After all you probably want to go out with as many as possible before you fall off your perch.

In effect your first date is always a blind date and make sure you go on it with a strategic escape route already planned which could include

A call from the Office

Grandmother suddenly ill

Son has locked himself out

Distant relative from Australia just arrived on your doorstep.

My date with Wendy was planned for the day after my return from holiday and I was a little apprehensive as this was a true blind date as I had not seen her photograph.

We had arranged for the usual pub lunch and would meet in the entrance. Just in case I had taken my own advice and had my strategic escape route planned.

First impressions were reasonably good, not bad looking, nice figure, reasonably well spoken but rather humourless and a bit severe looking.

Anyway we settled down with a drink and ordered the food. I was just about to open up the conversation when she started and after that I didn't get much opportunity to say a great deal.

She started off with a long and dreary diatribe about last year's hip replacement operation which was still giving her trouble and she was convinced the surgeon had got it wrong. I tried to make a medical joke at this stage as she had not smiled once since she arrived but it didn't seem to register at all. Then she started another long story about her cat and how she had to take it to vet with all sorts of ailments on a regular basis. I was beginning to get bored already and began to wonder if a good spanking would cheer her up, even at the risk of being called a sexual deviant, at least it could be fun.

Her next topic was the kitchen extension and all the trouble she had endured with the awful builder who used to get annoyed when she changed her mind at the last minute and then tried to charge her extra for the alterations. I almost felt sorry for the builder at this stage but was saved by the arrival of the food which at least filled her mouth and shut her up. I began to wonder if she liked oral sex as this could have the same effect.

Mercifully she ate her meal in near silence and didn't start up again until she had finished.

The next topic was her last holiday in Skegness with a woman friend and as if by magic photographs appeared from her handbag like a rabbit out of a hat. Looking at the pictures of them standing on a dreary flat windswept beach I began to lose the will to live. If I have to endure much more of this, I may contemplate suicide for the first time in my life so I decided to implement the exit strategy. I excused myself and popped off to the loo whereupon I phoned a friend so to speak and asked him to ring me back in exactly ten minutes' time.

I returned to the table refreshed in the knowledge that I would soon be saved, and the next topic was a forthcoming holiday with her friend to visit and take brass rubbings at all the churches in the area. Somehow I could envisage her moaning but unfortunately not in ecstasy, then the phone rang and I was saved. I explained that I had to take it as I was on call from work.

I pretended to have a conversation and expressed concern with a few "oh no's" and then said I would come right over and help to sort it out. I explained a friend had taken ill and

I had to go into work to replace him as a matter of urgency. I apologised profusely, said I would call her, left money on the bar and escaped at high speed.

It was a bit like the old joke about the girlfriend with child, when her Dad asks what steps you will take, the answer is "bluddy great steps in the opposite direction."

During the whole of our meeting she had never smiled once or asked me a single question.

INGRID THE I.T. ANORAK

Friday night was the big night on the internet when all the new profiles appeared and you could view the "new blood" with lusty interest as opposed to trawling through all the tired old ones in the hope that you missed a good one the third time around.

I settled down in the armchair with a large glass of wine and prepared to savour the moment. It always intrigued me to try to interpret what was said on the profiles to try and imagine the reality. For instance, "slightly overweight" invariably meant fat, a "full figure" probably meant enormous but I wasn't brave enough to find this out! Average appearance invariably meant ugly and looking for a casual relationship translated as sex.

I scanned through the massed profiles of divorcees, teachers, nurses and secretaries in the main and then my eyes alighted on Ingrid's profile as something a little out of the ordinary. An IT consultant, now that could be a useful lady to know the next time I have trouble with my anti-virus set up.

I fired off an opening message and sat back to await the results recalling that old saying around why computers have a feminine gender

No one but their creator understands their internal logic

The language they use to communicate with each other is incomprehensible to anyone else

Even the smallest mistakes are stored in the long term memory for possible retrieval at a later date.

As soon as you make a commitment to one you find yourself spending half your salary on accessories for it

They often don't function in the evening when the server is down.

Sure enough the next day I had a short reply and after a few more exchanges I asked her if she would like to meet and what she would like to do. She responded by saying she would like to meet up for a walk around the local reservoir and bring her dog with her. Sounds fine to me I thought so we arranged to meet in the reservoir car park. Thinking back, it wasn't the busiest spot in the world and she didn't know me from Adam so she was either being very brave or naïve, or possibly both.

I arrived a few minutes before time and parked up, shortly after she rolled up in a very trendy Chelsea tractor, otherwise known as a large 4x4 off roader. Unusual choice for an IT lady I thought but I would find out why later.

Ingrid was a pleasant looking woman with black framed glasses and a rather studious appearance. She could have passed as a slightly old fashioned schoolmistress in most company. She was dressed with an expensive casual sort of look and accompanied by a cute little mottled brown spaniel dog which had the rather appropriate name "Ginger"

My first impressions of Ingrid was that she was quite shy and would take a little getting to know, she seemed somewhat uncertain of herself and I got a kind of impression that she was not sure she wanted to be here. But, hey ho, the sun was shining and a five mile walk beckoned with ducks to feed so let's enjoy.

We set off with an excited Ginger straining at the leash and started to chat in a slightly disjointed way but she still seemed to be very shy and a little tense as if unused to male company although she was quite senior in her working life and must therefore mix with clients etc. I gradually started to draw her out and she began to tell me a little more about her life. She was brought up in a very strict conventional family with a Methodist background. She always had to dress modestly so as not to offend her parents and went to University in her home city so she could continue living at home and not be tainted by the wicked ways of the outside world. Post university she went into IT and had risen through the ranks in a major Company and now occupied a senior position in development. She had remained at home until in her thirties but then decided to move out to escape the increasing strictures of her ageing parents.

Ingrid had led a sheltered life and was somewhat naïve in matters of the heart. She had met a man at work who was in affect her first boyfriend and they had eventually married. Sadly, they were completely unsuited and the marriage fell apart after a year, with no offspring.

Ingrid admitted that she was very inward looking and had poor social skills, feeling uncomfortable in social gatherings. She put this down to sitting in front of a screen all day and communicating by e mail with limited face to face contact even with her work associates. Following her disastrous short lived marriage, she had become a bit of a recluse and spent most of her non work time at home. However, she knew she should really go out and try to meet someone before she got much older hence the internet dating agency.

Our walk in the sunshine nearly over we returned to the car park with a rather muddy Ginger who had managed to get covered in a type of thistle growing by the side of the path. Although she had told me plenty about herself she had not asked a single question about me. Whereas I said hello to everyone who passed by she never said a word to anyone.

However, on the basis of nothing ventured nothing gained and a feeling there could be something quite delightful just below the surface waiting to be released I asked her if she would like to visit me at home another day. Much to my surprise she invited me to her place instead and I took the address and we agreed on an evening the following week

Although she looked studious and bookish there was something about Ingrid which I found strangely attractive so I looked forward to our next meet.

Suitably after shaved and clutching a bottle of wine and a box of after eights I drove off to her village in some anticipation. After going up and down the main street several times I still could not find where she lived. Oh for Sat Nav I thought then I could get directions from a pleasant female voice guiding me across streams and up mountains.

Eventually I spotted a small track down the side of the tiny village shop and went down it. There was only enough width for one car and I could not make out if it actually led anywhere other than to a farmers' field. After half a mile of nothing I came across a small cottage on a bend in the track. It was all stone with a stone roof and a very pretty garden and I pulled over into a small parking area to go and ask for directions. I knocked on the door and lo and behold it was Ingrid who answered it. Did you find it OK she asked Yes of course, no problem at all I lied as we men hate to be thought of as useless navigators.

She looked very nice in a slightly old fashioned way and she had clearly made an effort as I could smell her lovely perfume as I greeted her with a chaste kiss. Even Ginger looked clean as she ambled over to give me a sniff and a lick.

The inside of the cottage was picture book, all oak beams, low ceilings, lots of brasses and an open fire burning real wood. Very cosy I thought; let's hope the evening lives up to its promising start.

We sat on cushions in front of the fire and sipped our wine, she was a bit more relaxed this time and probably somewhat more confident that I wasn't Jack the Ripper in disguise.

We drew closer and I could feel her heat and see the light from the fire dancing in her eyes as she looked into mine, this is going to be a great evening I thought; then it happened.

PPRRRPP the most fruity noise of slowly released flatulence, my God I thought what if she thinks it was me, it's bound to be a bit of a passion killer at the very least. I had better pretend it hasn't happened. For if I mention it and it was really her letting one slip out by accident, then she will be hugely embarrassed and it will spoil the whole evening.

So we resumed our by now slightly disjointed conversation until a few minutes later it happened again PPPRRRRRPPP but this time in overdrive and much louder and longer. We looked at each other with somewhat puzzled expressions and then a further short PPRRRPP gave the game away, it was coming from the corner where Ginger was lounging half asleep and looking very pleased with herself. We fell about laughing with considerable relief that it wasn't too embarrassing after all. When we had recovered Ginger was banished to the kitchen in a hail of air freshener and a vow never to feed her on liver and onions again.

We settled down once more to our cosy chat and enjoyed a gentle kiss and a roll around on the cushions. She was quite enthusiastic but not very skilful so I guessed she had not had a great deal of practice in the arts of Venus. My hand began to stray a little, as they do, to caress the outside of her generous breasts which she seemed to enjoy and her breathing quickened noticeably. As all was going so well I deftly undid a couple of buttons on her blouse, lifted her bra, and slid my hands in to warm them on her naked breasts and SHE FROZE. Unfortunately, the spell had been broken.

I apologised but thought she was comfortable with the situation. She looked me in the eyes and said don't worry it's not your fault. When the situation had subsided a little I questioned her some more and she told me that due to her strict religious upbringing she had great difficulty in letting go and enjoying sex in a normal way. She would reach a certain stage and then think of her parents or a preaching minister and that would just finish it for her. It was responsible for the breakdown of her marriage which had never been consummated fully for this reason. I asked her if she had sought help for this but she was too embarrassed to do so.

I asked her if a more gradual approach over a longer period of time might help but she thought not if her marriage was any indication.

This explained a lot of her contradictions to me as she seemed to want to meet men and yet was unsure of herself and what she wanted from them. It probably also explained why she led the life of a recluse and didn't seem confident in social situations.

I did feel really sorry for Ingrid and wished I could have gradually helped her to enjoy sex without anxiety and in a relaxed and pleasant way but sadly it wasn't to be. I still see her occasionally as we remain friends but its strictly brother and sister now.

FELICITY THE FEMINIST

I put my feet up with my customary glass of wine at the end of a busy working week and contemplated my navel. I thought women can drone on about uninteresting topics and you can actually dislike some of the women you date, but still you have a fascination with them. On the other hand, women have told me some real horror stories about the men they have dated. I guess it must be difficult for them once over the age of forty when it becomes harder to find a partner as there are fewer men who are unattached. It must be even more difficult to get one to marry you if they have already been screwed once in the divorce courts or are denied access to their children. Men may look for younger women; women will tend to look for a man of similar age, education and interests. Internet dating helps here but it may give too much choice allowing lots of dates but never the opportunity to get to know one person really well.

I then began to think about that most intimate part of a woman, it has always amused me that they don't seem to have a name for it themselves, or at least one that isn't rude. Many seem to refer to it as "down below" which could also mean the feet! What do you call it, my favourites are?

The perfumed Garden

Spam

Pussy

Fanoir

Antrum Amoris or cavity of love

But my undoubted favourite is "Royal enclosure – admittance to members only".

The phone rings and its Alan, a friend of mine who also enjoys a bit of internet dating but we don't talk about it much as we are normally in competition for the best prospects.

Richard, I have a challenge for you, I have recently been out with this gorgeous girl called Felicity, trouble is she's an ardent feminist; a real ball breaker and bunny boiler and I just can't make headway.

I know you like a challenge and I want to bet you £50 that you can't bed her. I thought about this for a few seconds and came to the conclusion that fortune favoured the brave or at least the slightly pissed and accepted the challenge.

Alan wished me luck and left me with her profile number. I looked it up; sure enough she was a fine looking girl, blond haired and petite, my favourite type. I read her profile and it was unusual to say the least. I could see what Alan meant and realised I would have to do some homework and research before tackling this challenge.

My research complete I decided on a course of action where I would be friendly, smiling and sympathetic but still capable of debating and criticising feminist issues in a nice way by the use of examples where necessary. I wrote my opening contact which I hoped would appeal, pressed the button and sat back.

Sure enough within a couple of days I had a rather guarded reply and thought I had better take the bull by the horns on this one and replied straight away. I told her that she looked very nice and was just the sort of girl I was hoping to meet and would she do me the honour (grovel, grovel) of having lunch with me.

Sure enough it worked and we arranged to meet the following week. I arrived in good time and thought I had better start off a little formal and with impeccable manners. She was a middle manager in a large company and arrived in one of those girlie creations where you press a button and the solid roof folds away. I made a mental note not to tell her that they are the most popular car among gays in France.

I made to open her car door but she clearly didn't want such help, she got out, dusted herself down and we shook hands rather formally. She was certainly a nice looking girl, let's hope my strategy works. When we went into the pub I held the door for her, which I would do normally for any woman, and she went through but instead of saying thank you she said "you don't need to do that". Ouch, prickly I thought!

When we sat down I pulled the chair out for her which, much to my surprise she accepted without comment, perhaps she is getting used to this I thought. I ordered drinks and we looked at the menu as this was the sort of place that cooked delicious food to order with nothing pre prepared. It took longer but was definitely worth it.

I opened the batting by asking how her week had been with a smile on my face and great interest in my eyes. She explained that business wise it had been very successful and as she was very focused and efficient she had met all the targets and only had one matter to resolve. She seemed a bit worried about this so I asked if she would share it with me as that may help her to deal with it (remember don't suggest any solutions unless asked).

She explained that a couple of nights ago she went to a leaving dinner which got a bit lively with copious amounts of alcohol flowing. One of her colleagues, a good looking guy, was sat across the table from her laughing and joking with those around him. He was normally a jovial sort but tonight for some reason she thought he was laughing at her and failed to see the joke. So she promptly got up and tipped an ice bucket over his head!!

Whoops I thought, we have a real bunny boiler here. Anyway this guy was a really nice easy going sort and didn't react which is probably just as well for her. However, she was not in favour with the rest of the staff the next day who thought she had reacted appallingly and she got a ticking off from her line manager.

This was a good entrée for me and I mentioned, without judgement, that I read in the paper the other day that 31% of women had had sex they didn't want while under the influence of alcohol. I went on to say that even when women behave drunkenly, coarsely and hunted half naked in packs they still expected to be respected and as a man I was confused by this. I wondered what had happened to decorum and good manners.

She took this in a remarkably calm manner but went on to justify the sisterhood by saying that men behaved badly and hunted in packs for sex so why shouldn't women. I agreed that I did not condone the behaviour of men either in this respect.

Good I thought it's warming up a bit, let's try another tack, as the old sailors say.

I asked her if she could help me with something (always a good opener) that had puzzled me for a long time. She agreed to do so and leant forward, always a good sign of interest.

I explained that as a widower, who had been out of the dating game for 30 years, I could understand many women needing to compete with men in the market place but I found women increasingly hard to please. On the one hand they seem to want someone to lean on, to look up to, as a companion and go to bed with but someone who knew his place in the post-feminist world nonetheless. At the same time, they want a man who can help with the household chores and cook but when you show capability in this respect and actually cook for them they tend to despise you and you begin to think is that what they really want.?

By this stage we were having a good friendly sparring contest; she was obviously a very bright woman and was turning out to be quite pleasant beneath that somewhat prickly exterior.

Our discussion was cut short by the arrival of the meal which looked absolutely superb, a fish bake with cheese for her and a steak and ale pie for me.

Eating gave me the time to review strategy and after the meal I asked what hopes and aspirations she had for the future. I suspect few people had ever asked her this before as she looked a little surprised. She started to look a little dreamy and said she might be embarrassed to tell me as we had just met. I explained that I used to be a sailor so very little embarrasses me, at which she smiled, wow.

For an alleged feminist she was remarkably conventional in her dreams and desires, she wanted a husband or at least a loyal caring partner, a nice house rather than a smart apartment and a happy fulfilled lifestyle. I remarked that I was sure she would find this but then she started to get slightly emotional by saying that she was having great difficulty in finding and keeping a man. She had plenty of first dates but few translated into second or subsequent dates. She also thought that her formal business persona and fairly high position at work also put men off and intimidated them somewhat. I thought, don't be tempted to give any advice at this stage Richard, or you will surely blow it.

I sympathised with her but only in very general nonspecific terms, looked her in the eyes and said that if she had enjoyed our first meeting I would be simply delighted to ask her out again. This seemed to have a profound and magical effect on her and she readily agreed and even started stroking my hand where it rested on the table. She seemed happy and relaxed and we spent the rest of the date in less serious mode telling the odd funny story and making her laugh. By the time I got home I had an e mail from her thanking me for a lovely afternoon, I was happy too, she was a very nice woman who perhaps needed to relax more and learn to enjoy herself.

There were quite a few other things I mentioned to Felicity during the course of our relationship and I have summarised these as follows:

Equal opportunities persuade women to pursue sex in the same way as men, but then men think no courtship is required.

The thrill of the chase for men is often negated by the easy capitulation of women and the drunken one-night stand.

Women's behaviour towards men is often governed by how they would like them to be in an ideal world, rather than how they actually are. Generally speaking, once over the age of 25 "what you see is what you get"

Forget booze, aggression, pack behaviour, political correctness, promiscuity and extreme feminism. This is no way to find a decent man.

Women want it all but they can't have it all. They want equal treatment in the workplace but special treatment when it comes to domestic life. It is usually the men who have to work late to meet the deadlines.

Men need to be strong, self-assured and confident. Feminists try to turn them into washing up wimps and then despise them.

In ancient times women yielded to the strongest men to get the best genes in their children. There is still a residual appeal of ravishment in women's minds, is that why they often date absolute bastards and still seem to enjoy it.

Don't forget even high earning feminist career girls can be soft and feminine given the opportunity. Don't forget all the supermodels bemoaning the lack of boyfriends as men were intimidated by their looks and earning power.

Finally, why do men who express a desire for submissive feminine women often end up marrying bossy, dominant, nagging and aggressive types?

Felicity and I had several further dates and we ended up in bed in her smart apartment. She turned out to be just the same as any other woman for she moaned, sighed and screamed at the same times. As we lay back in the afterglow she would chat to me about her hopes and dreams while I would concentrate on staying awake, like all men.

Sadly, it was not long before she was promoted and transferred to a far part of the country which gradually put an end to our relationship. She told me that one of the reasons for her promotion was that I had taught her to relax and to be more balanced in her views. I was pleased at her transformation and wished her well in her future.

I called Alan, mentioned that I had won the wager and suggested we met for a few beers and a curry as clearly we had some notes to compare. Besides by this stage I did feel in need of some uncomplicated male company.

The experience reminded me of the simple little definition of happiness

Happiness is

Someone to love

Something to do

Something to hope for

ALICE THE ANIMAL LOVER

It's always quite intriguing browsing through women's profiles and trying to see what they state they are looking for while at the same time speculating upon what they may be really looking for. The two are not the same, for instance "I am looking for someone to share life's rich tapestry" or "someone to share the good things in life with" does this mean to share things equally or hopefully enjoy a higher standard of living with a wealthy partner?

Similarly, "I am looking for that special person, who seems to be elusive", is the woman in question simply looking for Mr Perfect or setting an impossibly high standard?

Rather more honest and encouraging are the following

I am looking for someone to capture the joys of life with.

A caring personality to share a meaningful relationship.

Life is better when shared with someone.

I am looking for someone to laugh with.

To find a best friend and confidante.

But undoubtedly the most popular statement is along the lines of "to cuddle up in front of a warm fire with a glass of wine and the right person". A lovely idea I am sure we would all agree, but sometimes easier said than done, which brings me neatly on to my experiences with Alice.

Alice was a country girl, through and through and rarely visited towns except when she needed supplies, I was intrigued by her profile because although circumstances have made me a townie or suburban man, I have always had a desire to try the country life.

We arranged to meet in a nearby village for a bite to eat after which she promised to show me her small farm and animals, once she had satisfied herself that I wasn't a mass murderer or some kind of pervert.

I arrived a few minutes before the appointed time and had a walk around the village. Alice came trundling along in a rattly old Land Rover with a large dog in the back. She was dressed in jeans and wellies together with the typical country outdoor coat which was good quality but ten years old, battered and worn. She wore no makeup but was quite pretty and fairly tall with a nice looking figure no doubt earned from all the hard work on her farm. We greeted each other warmly and she was well spoken and obviously well educated.

We had met in a very unspoiled and original village where most people still earned their living from the land. She suggested the village pub to which I readily agreed and she opened the back door of her Land Rover and out bounded Buster a large and very friendly German shepherd dog. I made a big fuss of him and soon he was content to pad along beside us as we approached the porch leading to the pub. The entrance porch was one of these lovely original places with a flagstone floor and a row of farmer's wellies left there all stinking nicely of cow shit, very rural. As this was farming country there was absolutely no problem bringing your dog into the pub.

We entered and she greeted everyone in the way that everyone knows everyone else in the country. The place was about half full of farmers all having a lunchtime drink but it also appeared to have a small lunch menu chalked up on a blackboard behind the bar. I felt a bit self-conscious as the only townie in the place with my light weight clothing and somewhat dainty shoes. Every other person was attired in rugged country stuff that would no doubt survive years of abuse, rain, hail and cow shit.

We decided to order a plate of stew each in a big Yorkshire pudding together with a couple of drinks and then sat down for a chat.

It turned out that Alice at one stage had some sort of high flying job in the city but she eventually began to tire of the rat race and began to think there should be more to life. At about this time her elderly aunt had passed away and left her the small farm where she now lived. Alice often used to visit the farm as a child and loved helping with the animals and the general chores. Elderly aunt was obviously perceptive enough to know that she could enjoy it again and it would bring her back to her roots. So she made a decision, she was still single so she sold her London flat at a healthy profit, cashed in her investments, froze her pension and headed for the good life.

By this stage the food had arrived and what food, the plate was the size of a dustbin lid with a massive Yorkshire pudding in the middle and a great pile of hearty stew in the middle of the pudding. There was enough to feed two on each plate but that's country portions for you.

When we left the pub I was so full I felt and probably appeared to be six months pregnant but what food! Alice suggested leaving my namby pamby city car in the village as the track down to the farm was a bit rough and muddy, and so it was.

We turned off the main road and down this small track towards a lovely little stone house and barns with Buster barking excitedly behind us. As we bounced and lurched along we disturbed pheasants and other birds in the hedgerows, it looked simply idyllic, if a little isolated.

On the way down Alice was explaining that the reason she joined the dating agency was a distinct lack of suitable men in rural areas. She fell between two stools in the sense that she was educated to degree level and yet engaged in farming. So she wanted to find someone reasonably urbane and educated whereas most people she met were farmers who were tough hard working men but often with very limited formal education.

We entered her front door and the first thing I noticed was shabby furniture and bare flagstone floors. It should not have surprised me really as this was a working farm and such things were very practical. The next thing that hit me was the number of dogs and cats roaming around the place. There must have been six cats of all different colours and four dogs including Buster and I could really smell them. I always thought farm cats lived outside but Alice was a real animal lover. She took me on a tour of the farm and showed me her sheep and cattle which were some rare breed of which she was extremely proud. She also had goats, chickens, ducks on a small pond and some fantastic lop eared rabbits. She had created a vegetable patch and soft fruit area plus a small orchard with a large variety of fruit trees so was self-sufficient in many things. Surpluses were sold to local shops or bartered for other goods and as they were organically grown they were increasingly popular.

We were getting on like a house on fire by now and she explained that the farm just broke even but she was quite happy with this as it gave her the lifestyle that she wanted and she wasn't particularly materialistic. We opened a bottle of wine and sat down on the sofa to continue our conversation.

I could somehow sense that she was lonely and in need of company. She was modest, articulate, charming and very attractive in a natural sort of way. We toasted each other with our wine glasses and she moved slightly nearer. Her eyes sparkled and as I looked into those deep pools I knew this was a magical moment, my hand reached out and gently caressed her hair and her neck as we moved closer until our lips touched and we kissed. The intensity of our kisses grew at a furious pace and it was then that the dogs decided they would get in on the act and try to sit on our laps. OH BUGGER I thought but we just laughed it off. She explained that the only place the dogs were not allowed was in her bedroom and I responded by saying that I understood country people retired early of an evening. We climbed the stairs clutching the wine bottle and glasses and closed the door.

Neither of us said anything, we didn't have to, we knew what we wanted and what was to happen. I could tell she had not enjoyed the fruits of Venus for some considerable time and was keen to make up for the time she had lost. Later we lay together totally exhausted with the bed looking like a bomb site after our strenuous activities.

Lying back in the afterglow watching the sunset through the window I recalled that old song by Smokey entitled "Living next door to Alice" and whenever it was played in a pub everyone would sing the chorus line "who the …. Is Alice?"

Alice visited me a couple of times and although she enjoyed the sophistication of wine bars and trendy restaurants occasionally she did not enjoy the traffic and the busy town for she was a country girl at heart. Although we had daytime trysts she never stayed the night as she was tied to her farm and had to tend to the animals.

Eventually we realised that we had totally opposite lifestyles but I still see her occasionally. Who knows perhaps our lifestyles will converge a little more when we both retire.

MINTY THE MATRIARCH

Minty and I had the usual exchange of e mails and then decided to meet. She sounded like my kind of girl and we certainly appeared to have a lot in common. We spoke a couple of times on the phone and got on well. I arranged to pick her up from her home nearby and whisk her off to a nice country pub for lunch and a walk after.

She had a nice house with space around it, a rare commodity in England these days and I parked my convertible in the drive and rang the doorbell. I was a little surprised that she had invited me to her home on a first date as she didn't know me from Adam but apparently she was reassured by our telephone conversations.

She answered the door and greeted me warmly. She appeared to have put on a bit of weight since her profile photograph and maybe an extra chin but what the hell she seemed to have character and was warm and enthusiastic.

I settled her down in the leather seats of my convertible and off we roared to a little country pub I knew which served really good home cooked food. It was always heaving at the weekends but much quieter during the week.

We settled ourselves in at a window seat and ordered food and drinks then started to chat. Minty was an intelligent woman and we quickly became at ease with each other and had a good natural rapport. We had quite a lot in common; we had both been through the anguish of bereavement and had grown up children. We liked a lot of similar things and enjoyed a good laugh together.

After an excellent lunch we had a pleasant stroll around the village. I would have preferred a more exacting vigorous walk but got the impression this was not exactly her strong point or particular forte. I made a note to try her out on a five miler should the opportunity arise but the way things worked out this was not to be.

We drove home in the late afternoon and after a pleasant cup of tea and some vigorous snogging on a very large sofa I bade her farewell but not before we had arranged a second date for I thought she was very nice and she seemed to like me too.

Getting home with a spring in my step, because that is what romance does for you regardless of whether you are sixteen or sixty, I was really looking forward to our next meeting.

We had another successful outing after which we returned for tea and the sofa once again.

Resuming our vigorous snogging things got much steamier as I kissed her neck and nibbled her ears which seemed to drive her crazy, she was certainly one very sexy lady.

The temperature rose as I fondled her ample breasts and sucked and teased her prominent nipples with my tongue and by this stage she was getting very lively indeed. "Would you like to come to bed "she whispered in a very husky and sexy voice.

Now I am certainly no prude but I was a bit taken aback by this on only our second date. I usually catch up on all the women's issues and dictates on how men were expected to behave by reading all the magazines in my lady dentists waiting room. I distinctly remember reading a number of articles about not rushing or pressuring a woman in to bed too early in a relationship as she may think you are a sex maniac and do not respect her. I cannot recall that it gave any advice for men in similar situations and I was unsure how to respond. I decided to pretend I had not heard but to look forward and prepare myself for the third date.

Well on the third date and many others thereafter we always seemed to end up in bed after fifteen minutes on the sofa for appearances sake. Minty had an almost insatiable sexual appetite, was multi orgasmic and her entire body seemed to be one gigantic erogenous zone. She had a particular liking for oral sex and as all we men know each woman seems to have a particular smell and taste. Minty wasn't minty at all, more like a combination of deep forest moss combined with slightly stronger tree bark, rather earthy and primeval and, yes exciting. She would say dirty things, groan loudly, scream and her whole body would shake violently during orgasm, she certainly knew how to enjoy herself! She also enjoyed a bit of friendly domination where she would sit astride and above me while I played with her pendulous breasts and licked and teased her nipples in quick succession which would usually bring her to orgasm.

Minty also had her anxieties, she worried about her grown up children all the time and was terrified they would discover we were in a sexual relationship. She used to cluck over them like a mother hen despite the fact that some were married with kids of their own. Despite all this attention they were a very likeable bunch who had somehow achieved normality despite her attentions. I am sure they were often embarrassed by mother's attentions and knew exactly what we were up to, despite our innocent appearance.

Minty also had a little spaniel dog which was very friendly if somewhat fat and out of condition, she even had difficulty climbing two stairs. Every time I arrived she used to approach me all excited by the prospect of a good walk only to be disappointed when we took to the sofa.

Her husband had been a very successful and talented businessman who was the usual workaholic but at least he had left her well provided for. During his successful years she had grown used to being part of the "ladies who lunch" brigade wandering around rather aimlessly in a smart car and spending hubby's money while having the odd affair with business associates to relieve the boredom. Her ability to spend money, mostly on herself and her family, was unbelievable and seriously worrying in the long term.

It all happened rather quickly but we developed a serious relationship and a real love and affection, I hope we made each other happy, I think we did.

Nothing lasts forever and sadly it fell apart as quickly as it had happened, one day she just didn't seem to want me anymore and said she didn't love me. I was shocked by the suddenness, the callousness and the brutality of it but sometimes privilege breeds arrogance regardless of our rather more humble origins. Any woman who thinks that men are the only ones capable of this should think again.

Once something is done in this way there is no going back, I think it has sadly made me a little harder but perhaps the experience has done me good as I now realise that women can be hard and ruthless too despite being known traditionally as the weaker sex.

The saving grace is I am a tough character, I have had to be, and I mostly look ahead and not back. Perhaps Minty did me a favour and I will go on to meet someone who truly loves me and I her.

I suspect that with her family she had no room in her life for anyone else despite the fact that she was advertising for someone on the dating website. I hope you will feel the same way in five years' time, Minty, when they have all fled the nest and made their own lives.

BRENDA THE BIKER

Yes, it's Friday night once again and armed with a glass of wine I am perusing the new profiles and the women that have chosen me as one of their "favourites".

I glance through the profile of a very large lady who is offering me an alluring experience in bed and says she can hold her own and mine too if she likes me! Mm.

Although my search area is within 50 miles of my home town I have received a communication from Nanning in Guangxi province Central China which is stated to be 150 miles from England, better check the atlas, there may have been a significant seismic drift overnight that I am not aware of. The lady in question is 37 and has sent three very nicely but decently posed photographs of herself which is one more than the two lines of narrative on her profile. She is a makeup artist and looks very nice, but so does my passport.

Ah, now this looks promising, a lady called Brenda, nice photo, red haired and petite, lovely elfin smile and nice trim figure. Her photo showed her with nice dangly, slightly sparkly, earrings which really complimented her appearance and she had a generous pair of melons for her size.

As I read on I became even more intrigued as she described herself as a hippy rock chick into ethnic clothes and jewellery with a liking for classic rock particularly Jimmy Hendrix and

Led Zeppelin. She considered herself artistic, earthy, loving, open minded, sensitive, shy and unconventional. While she did not strike me immediately as long term material she did sound as if she could be a bit of fun. My interest grew as she went on to say she was sexy and affectionate and liked giving and receiving all kinds of massage. Wow, this one I have to meet.

Unfortunately, as I read on I didn't seem to qualify as she mentioned that she usually went for men with long hair, tattoos and motorbikes. However, there was a glimmer of impending maturity when she mentioned an intention to join the National Trust and visit a few stately homes.

Her favourite drink was mentioned as "Amarula" and for all I knew this could have been a type of anti-freeze beloved of smelly tramps. However, when I looked it up on the net I found that it was made from an African fruit found on the marula or elephant tree and harvested in the spring. The fruit is pulped to make a wine and then the solid residue is squeezed of juice which is added back to the wine to give it a distinct flavour. After two years of distillation the spirit is blended with fresh cream and bottled as "Amarula". I made a mental note to try her out on my unused bottle of "Amaretto di Sorono".

Amarula can be drunk on its own or blended into various cocktails, some of which go by the name of Monkey Brain, Orgasm, Skitso, Quick F-u-c-k and Slippery Nipples!!

Have you ever tried being a born again bikey? believe me it's a really frightening experience not to be repeated. Traffic volumes have increased tenfold since I rode regularly and you just feel so vulnerable after being in a car. You are kitted out like the urban spaceman and feel claustrophobic in an enclosed helmet. No other road users seem to see you which can give you some close shaves and women drivers in particular pull out in front of you or decide to do a three point turn around bends in country lanes. A two seater sports car is equal fun but you are just likely to live longer.

Anyway I decided I was going to have a bit of fun with this one so I sent off a nice message explaining I used to have a bike until I had an accident, not an unusual occurrence in bikey circles. I also mentioned that I had a few tattoos and would grow my hair longer and dye it black just for her. After a couple of days, I had a nice response saying that although I wasn't her usual date I sounded nice and she would make an exception for me.

After a couple more messages we arranged to meet in a bikey pub on the edge of town and I started to worry a bit about my lack of tattoos. I then had the bright idea of inviting a lady friend of mine around for a drink as she ran a beauty salon and I asked her to bring her box of tricks with her, explaining what I needed. She thought it was an absolute hoot and joined in the fun wholeheartedly.

In the meantime, I thought about my distant days in the Royal Navy and the wide variety of tattoos displayed by sailors. The most magnificent one was the scene taking up most of the lower back and the buttocks which depicts a hunting scene where the horsemen and hounds are pursuing a fox which is disappearing down the crack of the buttocks. However, the most exotic one was a thin blue line down the penis which must have been extremely painful to have done. Rumour had it that when the said member was in an excitable state the thin blue line read "SASKATCHEWAN".

I decided that this was too complicated in the time available as my date was the following day so I popped into the local theatrical shop. I hadn't really looked around this place before but it was a veritable treasure trove and I selected a large gold coloured clip on gypsy earring and some transfer tattoos to add to the street cred.

My friend duly arrived and I decided on a dotted blue line around my neck with "cut here" written just below the Adams apple. I had "mild" and "Bitter" inscribed just above each of my nipples and a couple of anchor transfers, one on each forearm. This left the transfer of a rose which I explained to my friend I intended to fix to my left buttock using a mirror. She told me not to be so shy and much to my surprise and slight embarrassment told me to drop my trousers and promptly fixed it for me. I thanked her profusely and suggested that we should go out for dinner sometime, never look a gift horse in the mouth, that's what I say!

The day dawned for my lunch date so I donned my old leather jacket and drove off to the pub but was careful to leave the car parked around the corner. It was a typical scruffy, slightly down at heel bikey hang out complete with snooker and pool tables. There were a few bikes outside and a few guys inside playing a lethargic game of pool. I wandered in with my hands firmly wedged in my pockets and there she was at the bar having a drink and a crafty fag. Her red hair shone, her smile was every bit as good as her photographs and even before I met her I could feel a primeval stirring in the loins, she was turning me on before we had even said hello.

After the usual greetings and a polite kiss on the cheek I gave her a single red rose which went down extremely well,

I don't suppose bikeys do that kind of thing but all women seem to enjoy a bit of chivalry. I ordered drinks, amarula for her and wine for me and suggested we take a table. She got down from her bar stool and her short skirt rode up to reveal a tantalising momentary glimpse of black panties. She was only about 5ft 2 inches tall with a really trim figure and dangly sparkly ethnic earrings. I walked over to the table with some difficulty and sat down with great relief. We started to chat and got on extremely well together. After the third round of drinks I began to worry about having the car with me and suggested we order some food. It was typical bikey fare, anything you want providing it comes with a hamburger and chips.

We toasted each other with our drinks and looked into each other's eyes. I could tell she was hot and so was I, moving forward slowly and gently I put my hand on her shoulder and drew her to me kissing her gently on the lips like the kiss of a butterfly. She responded well and she wanted more, things were getting quite steamy when the food arrived. We ate the meal in almost total silence looking into the pools of each other eyes, for we both knew what would happen next.

She asked me if I would like another drink but I explained I had the car with me so she said, why don't we just have another and I will show you where I live, it's just around the corner. It did not take long to finish that drink and off we went arm in arm to her place for the grand tour. The house was small but lovely and full of her art work plus the odd photo of presumably former boyfriends astride various hogs. We finished the tour in her bedroom where she sank on the bed and patted the side inviting me to join her. By this stage I needed no encouraging and we writhed on the bed in a frenzy of passion while desperately trying to remove each other's clothes at the same time. She had a gorgeous body which I kissed all over and she also loved oral sex which gave her several strong orgasms before the main event. Our lust temporarily slated we opened a bottle of wine and lay together in a contented afterglow. Later we massaged each other before starting all over again.

I didn't leave until nine the following morning, starving hungry and totally exhausted, but what a night and she even admired my rose tattoo. I got home, ate a cowboy's breakfast and fell into a sleep of deep contentment.

POSSESSIVE PIPPA

It's always interesting when you invite a woman to visit your house. I would not suggest this on the first date or she may think that you are intent on showing her the bedrooms. Once you have gained her confidence her natural curiosity will take over and she will be keen to see just how and where you live. Of course a certain amount of preparation is necessary; those crusty old socks will need to be put away and a general tidy and clean-up is advisable. The impression you need to give is of someone who is organised and can cook and keep a tidy house. The ideal balance is to have a house with a standard of cleanliness and orderliness which is very acceptable but just below her standards so you are perceived as being competent and only in need of slight improvement. Whatever you do don't get fanatical about cleanliness otherwise you may exceed her standards and create too much competition for her.

Women love to have a nosey around and check out the décor and the ornaments. If you have any ornaments of an erotic nature acquired in places such as Thailand and Fiji showing improbably large endowments for instance it may be advisable to put them in a cupboard for the first visit as they could frighten her.

This is the ideal opportunity to show that you are a discerning man of impeccable taste and do make sure that you have a good selection of pictures and paintings on the wall which will add to her interest and make sure you know something about them so that you can talk with confidence and authority. If you have a number of sex manuals in your bookcase and copies of Viz and porn magazines on your coffee table, hide them away and replace with a boring but impressively sized tome on the History of Art.

If you really want to make an impression you could even clean the loo and hang one of those nice smelling disinfecting things in the bowl and put one of those pink silly frilly things around the spare bog roll. You could also consider encasing your box of tissues in something similar and finally purchasing a large arrangement of dried flowers to be placed in a position where it looks really pretty but constantly gets in your way.

Her reaction to your house will be interesting. If it is better than hers she will probably enthuse and say how beautiful it is and how you are so lucky to live in it. She may even go so far as to say that she would love to live in a place like that.

On the other hand, if she has a similar or even better place she will be complimentary but not quite as enthusiastic as clearly it is of the standard she is used to.

A word of caution here, simple good manners would dictate that once she has had a good look at your place it would be polite for you to be invited to her abode within the next couple of meetings. If she does not be extremely wary for if she lives in a shoebox she could prepare you for it beforehand. It is however very likely that she has something to hide which could be

A husband or travelling lover

An old granny dribbling in the corner

A Great Dane 4-foot-high at the shoulder

A couple of kids she just forgot to mention

A female lodger with shaven head wearing dungarees

Her 40-year-old brother who has never married and who has an unhealthy interest in things on washing lines

A lot of friends who pop in dressed in yellow robes and ringing little bells.

A word of warning to my more mature readers, if you have the benefit of a good pension it is best not to mention it at all as less scrupulous women could see it as a meal ticket for life. If you are the sort of man that thinks Fidelity is something to do with insurance, then the risk factor is increased by at least 100%.

Which brings me neatly to Pippa, nice profile and attractive looking and well worth making contact with, so I did. I suppose many women are conditioned by the experiences they have with men on the internet dating scene. There is evidence to suggest that many have some bad experiences and they then believe that all men act the same. Be that as it may I was still not prepared for what was about to happen.

We had a very nice exchange of e mails and found out that we both lived in the same town. I hadn't heard from her for about three weeks and had begun to wonder if she had found someone else when out of the blue a new message arrived. This implied that she had not received a message from me and I had obviously been put off by her description of our town as a large village. Needless to say I was very puzzled by this but the implication seemed to be that I had not made contact because I was somehow worried we may know the same people and perhaps I was also dating one of her friends. As I had not even been out with her at this stage this was absolutely none of her business anyway. In her next few messages I thought I was being interrogated and she seemed to be trying to catch me out for some reason. I began to feel very uneasy about this woman but decided that maybe a meeting would clear the air.

I thought neutral ground would be best so stuck to the conventional pub lunch. She drove into the car park and I stepped forward to say hello and open the door for her. She was very nice looking, petite with dark hair, well dressed and well spoken. We had an excellent lunch and got on extremely well together and enjoyed a good laugh. Maybe I have judged her wrongly I thought, for she seems entirely normal. We parted company in the late afternoon sunshine and we arranged to contact each other later to arrange another meet.

Imagine my surprise when a few days later an e mail arrived telling me that I did not seem to be available evenings and weekends and this can only mean that I am involved with another woman and am playing the field. I was really quite amazed considering that I was not in a relationship with this woman and had had one lunch with her and kissed her on the cheek when saying farewell.

One of the key aspects of dating is that you go out with many to try to find your soul mate but in reality you only have a relationship with the few to whom you are attracted and feel you have a lot in common with. This is part of the natural selection process but to have a woman who is so controlling and possessive before you have even entered into a relationship is an extremely worrying development. In reality I could not face continuing this relationship as imagine what it would be like if you were in an intimate relationship with this woman.

I am never sure if women really understand the sort of actions that drive men away so I have attempted to summarise them as follows:

ACT SWEET THEN CHANGE WHEN YOU HAVE HIM.

The sexy nightie is replaced with a flannelette one and a set of curlers (face cream optional).

She dresses like she doesn't care anymore.

Every day is a bad hair day.

Figure getting bigger

Man feels he has been duped

NOT GIVING ENOUGH SPACE

Clings to you to ensure you are not fooling around

No room to be yourself or hang around with your friends

Letting a man out of their sight is a mistake

WANTING TOO MANY THINGS

They want a standard of living you cannot afford

They moan and complain if they cannot have it

If the man is content with what he has he is being complacent, lazy and lacking ambition

NOT SAYING WHAT SHE MEANS

Men are not good at working out what a woman means

Women are far more sophisticated communicators

Women understand subtle gestures and body language much better than men

Some women do not express themselves honestly and openly

Women can be saying one thing when their body language conveys the opposite

Men often miss nonverbal signs

SEX

Men complain about lack of enthusiasm, no creativity and poor technique

Men complain of boring sex with no variety, more of a duty than a desire

Using sex as a weapon angers men

A man cannot expect a woman who is angry at him to want to make love

Communication is important

CONSTANTLY TALKING ABOUT OTHER MEN

Men don't like to hear women talking about other men as each man wants to feel special

Male ego can be fragile

BEING A DRAMA QUEEN

Always whining, pestering or nagging about something, nothing can ever be right

Always trying to obtain and control a man's attention

Tries to plan every hour of every day for him

Plays the damsel in distress card

BEING HARD AND COLD

Openly disrespectful, aloof, non-communicative

Men have feelings and this kind of behaviour drives them away

When the home environment is colder and tougher than the work environment then there is little solace

CHEATING

Common to both sexes

Physical cheating by having an affair

Mental cheating by trying to get one over on him and trying to control him

THE POWER STRUGGLE

Men get annoyed when women are constantly trying to upstage them

Particularly annoying for men who don't compete with their mates

Women now engage in power struggles with their mates over career advancement, education etc.

Women try to make themselves look smarter than a man by intentionally upstaging him in public

They disagree for the sake of it

Women can be extremely rude and expect to get away with it

They can be condescending and can cut down what a man says

Thankfully although I have experienced an extremely possessive woman I have yet to encounter a stalker!

IN PRAISE OF THE MORE MATURE WOMAN

Women of a certain age are so different from their mothers and if they have been wise, can live a totally different lifestyle. Let me explain, they probably had fewer children and were therefore not quite as worn out with child bearing and child raising. They probably worked at some stage during the process of child raising and therefore created and retained interests outside the home. They were likely to be more affluent with a greater awareness of lifestyle, nutrition and the need for exercise. As a result of this they approach retirement age with better health, trimmer figures and a wider range of interests, often including a healthy desire for both sex and companionship.

As retirement looms many will enjoy better health, wealth and education than their mothers ever did. Most will have the family off their hands by this stage and be free to enjoy leisure time, travel and whatever else they fancy. They may be used to significant independence and be personally confident with a wide circle of friends but many will still yearn for that special friend, a man to share their lives with, in some shape or form. This may not be the conventional state of marriage for after all, the need for security and legitimising children has long since gone and a number of new possibilities arise. I know people who live together, others that simply visit each other's houses from time to time. Some women are quite happy to cohabit when travelling or on holiday when a companion can be desirable to share and enjoy the experiences. Many women may want their own space some of the time and a soul mate for the remainder.

Most women however do feel a strong need to be appreciated, desired and to

feel alive in the company of a man, hence the demand for dating services. By retirement age far more men than women remain married often due to different mortality rates and therefore choice could be limited in a locality. However, with the advent of dating services far more theoretical choice at least has been created. Whether this choice translates into real relationships remains to be seen as too much choice can lead to indecision and women's standards and requirements have been raised over the years.

Undoubtedly the biggest liberator for women though is the freedom from childbirth, contraception and hopefully PMS as they grow gracefully older.

This will come as a great relief to many men too as there are certain days in the month when a man has to tread very carefully indeed and here is my guide to survival at this time.

RECKLESS What's for lunch?

SAFE   Can I help you with lunch?

SAFEST   Where would you like to go for lunch?

BEST   Here, have some chocolate

RECKLESS Did you get that at the Oxfam shop?

SAFE   You look really nice in pink and green

SAFEST   You look lovely

BEST   Here, have some chocolate

RECKLESS What are you so angry about?

SAFE   What have I done wrong?

SAFEST   Would you like £50 for that new dress?

BEST   Here, have some chocolate

RECKLESS   Should you be eating that?

SAFE   There is some salad left in the fridge

SAFEST   Would you like a glass of wine with it?

BEST   Here, have some chocolate.

RECKLESS What did you do all day?

SAFE   I hope you didn't do too much today

SAFEST   I have always loved you in that flannelette
              nightie.

BEST   Here, have some more chocolate.

For those men out there totally confused by PMS, and there must be many, here are some definitions to help you along:

PMS THESAURUS

Pass my shotgun

Psychotic mood shift

Perpetual munching spree

Puffy mid-section

People make me sick

Provide me with sweets

Pardon my sobbing

Pimples may surface

Pissy mood syndrome

Plainly, men suck

Pack my stuff.

Of course not all the world's problems are caused by PMS, here are a selection of problems women encounter with men when dating

Never Listen (what did you say?)

Don't show any respect

Talk about themselves all the time

Lucky to find a man who can remember where he has left his teeth.

Doing you a favour by going out with you

His idea of getting lucky was finding his car in the supermarket car park

Unfortunately, I never realised that the penis shrinks by 20% as a man grows older (neither did I)

Of course there are distinct advantages in going out with a mature woman and here are some of them for your delectation

A mature woman is a cheaper date as instead of downing a dozen beers like her younger counterpart she usually gets sufficiently squiffy on a couple of glasses of wine.

Mature women can run faster as they wear more sensible shoes

Mature women are more honest, if you are a twat they may call you one as they are less worried about a relationship breakdown.

A mature woman will never get pregnant and demand marriage.

A mature woman can take charge of a situation and has confidence

A mature woman knows how to cook; a younger woman knows how to call the take away.

A mature woman will introduce you to all her girlfriends, a younger woman will not just in case you stray.

A mature woman often has a rather shocking lingerie collection.

A mature woman has confidence, dignity and is hopefully less possessive.

A mature woman has lots of girlfriends, many of whom may be attracted to you.

A mature woman will never accuse you of stealing the best years of her youth because someone else has stolen them first.

So now you understand the mature woman a little better than you did before, here are my dating tips

Age is not really that important, it's just a number

Compatibility, open communication and respect are important

She may be confident and have good communication and conversational skills but remember she may be just as nervous on a first date as she was at sixteen.

Be complimentary about her clothes or hairstyle.

Make her feel beautiful, she may be anxious when comparing herself to younger women.

Point out her best features, but please be tasteful.

Show good humour and interest in her so she feels relaxed.

Remember she may have had bad dating experiences in the past.

Check discreetly in conversation what sort of baggage she is carrying.

Be a gentleman at all times, take things a little slower to reflect an older style of values.

Ensure that you come across as educated, smart, refined and very presentable when meeting her friends.

ENJOY!!

WHAT ARE MEN REALLY LOOKING FOR

Whatever it is it will probably be different to women's desires. My usual exhaustive survey revealed the following top four in order of priority.

WARM/SENSITIVE/CARING

Men seem to crave a warm and caring woman but often what they seem to get is cold, selfish and demanding. After a hard day at work they like to relax and chill out in the warmth and love of their family. They crave to be accepted for what they are and what they were when they established the relationship. They don't take very kindly to being compulsorily improved or moulded into the shape and style which their partner believes they should be in an ideal and perfect world.

EASY GOING/BEST FRIEND

Similar to 1 in a way, men hate to be nagged over trivia in particular. They may not want to put up the shelves of an evening after work and may wish to do it at the weekend instead. Very few women appear to be really easy going and most seem to nag from time to time.

Men often really want a best friend; they hate demanding hostility which many get in relationships. They prefer someone who loves them for what they are.

LOYAL/TRUSTWORTHY/HONEST

Goes without saying and a high scoring attribute with women too.

GENTLE/KIND/SINCERE

These qualities are highly prized by women too.

A WORD ABOUT BUNNY BOILERS

The phrase came to prominence in a well-known film and is used generally to describe women who are difficult to deal with and who may exhibit some or all of these characteristics

Wild mood swings

Extreme behaviour

Desperation to retain a failing relationship

Occasional violence/violent outbursts

Very demanding and vindictive

Extremely jealous and possessive

Will take revenge after a failed relationship

Will damage your possessions in fits of rage

Will boil your pet rabbit and serve it up as the evening meal as revenge for whatever you did or didn't do.

Obviously this is an extremely dangerous species for the average man to deal with and great care is required even when approaching one socially or informally. Think of it as the equivalent of dancing with a hungry cobra and whatever you do, don't get involved regardless of how pretty she is. Stick with one that meets the criteria under 1 and 2 above and you will be much happier. You also get to keep your pets!

If you have a new woman in your life and you are worried about potential tendencies you can try my Bunny Boiler Test, set out below. Just score each answer according to the number alongside each of your answers and the analysis is at the end of the survey.

THE BUNNY BOILER TEST

Question 1

You leave a rather crusty pair of used socks on the

bedroom floor

Does she

1. Pick them up and put them in the laundry basket.

2. Nag you about them

3. Pick them up and drop them in your cornflakes

Question 2

You go shopping and wait outside the changing room doors while she tries a dress on. She comes out and catches you ogling a couple of bits of jail bait.

Does she

1. Smile sweetly, knowing all men do this.

2. Complain that you never give her as much attention

3. Denounce you as a pervert and call store security to evict you.

Question 3

You ask her how she dealt with the ending of her last relationship and she replies

1. We knew we were not right for each other and parted

good friends

2.   We had a blazing row, I called him a lazy no good bastard and I walked out.

3.   I accused him of dumping me and made all his suit trousers into shorts before I left.

Question 4

You are watching a horror film together involving a mad knifeman, does she

1.   Avert her eyes and express her dislike

2.   Nag you to watch a romantic film instead.

3.   Seem totally absorbed and really enjoying it.

Question 5

You are at a friend's wedding reception enjoying chatting up all the bridesmaids and she approaches, does she

1.   Smile and introduce herself as your partner

2.   Complain to all around that you never chat to her like that.

3.   Pour a glass of wine over your head and glare at the other girls.

Question 6

At the wedding reception a man squeezes her bottom when passing, does she

1.   Smile at him, say you thought he was gay, in a very loud voice.

2.   Tell him if he does that again she will empty the trifle bowl into his trousers.

3.   Drop kick him in the balls with her stiletto heels.

Question 7

You return home slightly confused after a lad's night out and try to go to sleep in the wardrobe. Does she

1.   Help you undress and get you into bed.

2.   Tell you off and insist you sleep in the bath just in case you are sick.

3.   Threaten you with a kitchen knife for disturbing her sleep at 3am.

Question 8

You have become obsessed with your tropical fish collection and have been neglecting your partner, does she

1. Try to take an interest in it.

2. Complain that you think more of them than her.

3. Serve them up with chips and a glass of tank water.

Question 9

She comes home one day to find you have left a bunch of roses on the bed for her, does she say

1. Oh, how thoughtful and romantic.

2. He is feeling guilty, what has he been up to.

3. That bugger has been playing away again, I will stick these up his …. when he gets home, complete with thorns.

Question 10

She finds the card for a lap dancing club in your suit pocket when taking it to the cleaners, does she

1. Ask why you went there and what it was like.

2. Complain that's where all the housekeeping money is going.

3. Refuses to speak, sleeps in spare room and organises a male stripper party for all her mates.

Question 11

A strange woman you befriended in a nightclub keeps calling when you are out and your partner is suspicious, does she

1. Ask if it is a business associate.

2. Accuse you of being up to your old tricks again and demand an explanation.

3. Trace the number, ring her back and threaten to break her legs.

Question 12

You return from the office Christmas party at 3.30 am rather the worse for wear, carrying a traffic sign, wearing a funny hat, lipstick all over your shirt, a cold pizza in one jacket pocket and a pair of very used knickers in the other, does she

1. Ask you if you had a good time team building.

2. Complain that this happens every year and you shouldn't drink so much.

3. Take you to the office at 10 am when everyone is nursing monumental hangovers; waive the knickers in the air and demand to know who they belong to, in an extremely loud voice.

Now if the love of your life scored between 12 and 16 she is a little jem. Love her, cherish her and give her a big bunch of roses without trying to look too guilty.

Between 16 and 24 you probably have a fairly normal woman and may wish to concentrate on getting her scores down a bit.

Between 24 and 36 you may have a Bunny Boiler and you should devise a subtle and cunning escape plan just in case. Could I suggest an escalating involvement with the Princes Trust in their project to restore an all-male Greek Monastery up the side of a mountain on a remote Greek island where women are not allowed. At least you should be safe there.

WHAT ARE WOMEN REALLY LOOKING FOR

After exhaustive research and a mammoth survey, I have come up with the top ten attributes that women seem to want in a man, in the following priority order

LOYAL/TRUSTWORTHY/HONEST

Far and away the most important attribute for women by a very large margin.

WARM/ SENSITIVE/ CARING

Not always obvious male attributes but seen as important in a relationship.

EASY GOING/ BEST FRIEND

This seems to stem from women's need to have that "special person" in their lives.

FUNNY/MAKES ME LAUGH

Going by the many books and articles I have read I would have expected this to be higher.

Others in priority order were

Gentlemanly/kind/sincere

Romantic/enjoys the good things in life

Positive outlook/adventurous

Not afraid of commitment

Young at heart/outgoing

Articulate and intelligent

The ladies in the survey also pointed out that I had forgotten about the following

Looks and physique

Not too hairy

Nice bum

And who can argue with that!

Regardless of how independent they may appear; most women seem to have a huge desire to share their lives with a special person but sadly it doesn't always work out that way.

Here is what many of them say

I need someone special to share things with

Nothing is that good unless you are sharing the experience

I want a soulmate who understands and cares for me

It's good to share your life with someone; you have more fun and get more out of it

Someone to capture the joys of life with

Things are better shared with the right person

I really don't know what to do with myself

I miss that special person to come home to

Here are some of the stranger statements found on women's profiles together with my comments:

They tell you what they like and don't like to eat I am a dessert specialist check size on profile

I want someone at least 5ft 10 inches. why, when you are only 4ft 11 inches tall

Must have sparkling eyes is Gary Glitter still available

My family think I am mad oh really

I still haven't found Mr Right, where are you hiding

They all like eating but few offer to cook for you I have cooked for more

I have asked my friends to describe me don't you know yourself

I wish I could date myself as I would be the perfect match for me no comment

I like to try anything new really, can I have your tel. no

Guess I am looking for a male version of me is anyone out there? I doubt it

I need to meet my male equivalent careful he might be gay

I sing to my dog and make up crazy rhymes don't call me, I'll call you

I will dig a big hole outside my door and wait for a man to drop in what was your address again

I am a 53-year-old nutty tart who feels half her age what sort of nuts do you like

I am here to meet people, not collect pen pals bunny boiler

I need to trust a normal man with no hang ups or sexual deviances counts me out then

Personality and a good sense of humour are more important than looks although a Quasimodo look alike is pushing things a bit sorry, I've got the hump

Looking for a male version of myself, according to friends that's going to be completely impossible they are right

I am told I can talk the hind leg off a donkey and I am a big handful really! how big?

I am looking for a man who knows how to open another bottle of red without being asked piss artist

I really love walking but I have no sense of direction at all Where are you?

I have had my share of frogs, now looking for a Prince to

love he may have croaked

He must be house trained and like DIY It's a man she wants, not a dog

I am bald but very attractive so is one of my male friends

I could go on for ages but I am not going to thank God

I am overweight, middle aged, average appearance and separated are those your good points?

I am an extrovert introvert- thank you, vodka and **diet coke please, better make it a large one**

He must be a dog lover as I have 5 is there any room in your house?

I have learned to take spiders out of the bath myself you ought to meet my pet tarantula

Heavy boozing and gambling is a definite no no, nerdy blokeish hobbies just acceptable, but not train spotting

For once I don't know what to say

According to serious newspapers men are not attracted to:

Women who can I have a job description and an application form please together with a vision and mission statement

1 Are independent, practical and capable 2 Are highly educated

3 Are quick witted and able to tell a joke

I am all of these things and proud of it

One man even recommended that I play dumb to get a mate!!

I'm physically fit

        built like an Amazon and can beat you at arm
        wrestling

I like men's hobbies

        could be a cigar smoking lesbian

I'm a free spirit

    hasn't shaved her legs since 1995

I live a healthy natural lifestyle

    dreadlocks, sandals, she will make you eat
    stuff which looks like building materials only
    suitable for goats

I'm a confident girl who knows what she wants

    she wants ridiculous things such as flowers
    three times a week and a card on her dead
    cat's birthday

I want someone I can share every moment with

    she insists on being no more than three feet
    away from you every single moment of your
    life

I am open to experimentation in the bedroom

    no matter what you are into, she is far ahead
    of you

I'm a little girl at heart

> once she moves in you will find hearts and
> teddy bears everywhere watch out for the
> scented candles and dolls on your coffee
> tables

I practice (some weird) religion

> you will be persuaded after a couple of
> weeks to join some strange cult, dress in
> bright robes, ring a bell and collect money
> in shopping centres you could end up in an
> army style camp in the Orkneys working for
> nothing, having donated all your worldly
> goods to the cause

Finally, do be wary if a woman sends you a black and white photograph of herself as this may have been taken some time ago.

If she sends one of her clutching her pet hound or hounds, you may have to pass the

ANIMAL TEST

If you date her and manage to get back to her place be very careful as you will almost certainly face the animal test and if they don't like you there is simply no hope. Whatever you do, do not display hostility, tell the thing to bugger off or be tempted to give it a sly kick or all will be lost. So just sit there on the sofa and relax with your cup of tea while the little doggy tries to shag your left leg and leaves unmentionable stains on your trousers and deposits in your turn-ups. Your host will probably exclaim that he really likes you and isn't as friendly with everyone. Cats take a little more time to get to know you but at least they don't try anything like that.

HOW DO MEN AND WOMEN CHOOSE EACH OTHER

With great difficulty of course but there is an increasing trend to be scientific rather than intuitive? For instance, I sat a woman friend of mine down with a very large glass of wine and asked her to assume she had an internet message from a man and to describe to me how she would deal with it. This was her selection process, at the end of each action she can accept or reject him

Look at photo

Accept or reject

No photo

Reject

Would I kiss him?

Is he looking at a very wide age range?

Is he too young/old?

Is child status ok

How tall

How far away does he live?

How does he write and spell?

Does he appear to be at least as intelligent as I?

Does he have a good sense of humour?

Does he seem to have nice manners?

If anyone is left after this selection, then a date is arranged

After first meeting   Accept/reject

Is there anyone out there?

Staying for the moment with men's issues, here are your ten tips for a successful first date.

THE 10 TIPS

1. Take a bath or shower, clean your teeth and have a shave. Women are more fastidious in these things, other than shaving of course.

2. Arrive on time. Shows reliability

3. Give her a little gift. A single rose or small piece of chocolate.

4.   Be a gentleman. Hold doors open for her, pull her chair out etc. She will feel special and by treating her like a lady you will gain copious brownie points. Be yourself, don't try and pretend you are someone you are not.

5.   Compliment her. Tell her she is beautiful and is wearing a lovely dress but don't overdo it and whatever you do don't tell her she has breasts like a pair of ripe melons, this may not go down too well at this stage.

6.   Listen to her and ask questions. Take an interest in what she has to say and make sure you look her in the eye and not the melons! Let her talk more than you do as this is a natural state and if you get a little bored try to take a crafty glance at her melons. Make her feel comfortable and relaxed, she may be a little nervous on first meeting.

7.   Prepare for the conversation. Ask her questions about herself and make sure you have read the paper before meeting so you can discuss a wide range of topics. Avoid talking about past relationships. Inject humour and laugh with her. Be confident and protective.

8.   Pay for the date. If you have asked her out always pay for it as an act of chivalry. If you both want to meet again there is no problem her paying for the second date if she offers. Consider an alternative to the usual meal such as a fun fair or stately home tour.

9.   The goodnight kiss. Most women will be reasonably comfortable with this and if the date has gone well, possibly enthusiastic. However, do not attempt to

ram your tongue down her throat and definitely do not try to grope any prominent bits at this stage in the proceedings.

10. I will call you. Only tell her you will call if you intend to. Otherwise say it was nice meeting you and wish her luck.

Now chaps if you get that lot right you should be doing quite well but here are a few pointers on what not to do

1. Talk about yourself all night.

2. Eat with your mouth open.

3. Ask lots of personal questions.

4. Forget to thank them for the date.

5. Get drunk or talk about sex.

There is an increasing trend for internet daters, both men and women, to use profile headers to catch your attention and make them stand out from the herd. Here are a few of the strangest and funniest ones I have encountered –

Some will, some won't, some do, some don't, I might.

I hope you want a cavity.

A positive attitude may not solve all your problems, but it will annoy enough people to make it worth the effort.

Ashes to ashes; dust to dust; life is short, so party we must.

Sensi the night dragon drifted through the sky, her beautiful fragrance charmed those in her wake.

If only a closed mind came with a closed mouth.

I never grow old because I drink from waterfalls.

Did you know that 1 in 12 kids get their heads stuck in a bucket?

I'm the love pirate and I'm here for your booty.

My prince took the wrong turn, got lost, and was too damn stubborn to ask for directions.

Drinking coffee out of plastic makes you impotent.

Whenever I feel blue I start breathing again.

I don't suffer from insanity; I enjoy every minute of it.

I want to meet a guy whose IQ is bigger than his shoe size.

Looking for a man with a very large bulge in his back right pocket.

I like my men to be like my bra – supportive.

Love is a sweet dream and marriage is the alarm clock.

Ready for the three ring circus, engagement ring, wedding ring, suffering.

Girls are like phones. They like to be held and talked to, but if you press the wrong button you'll be disconnected.

Since light travels faster than sound, is that why some people appear bright until they speak.

I believe in dragons, good men, and other fantasy creatures.

Willing to lie about how we met.

Take me to the moon; I'm not a halfway kind of girl.

Just like a new job, I offer excellent benefits.

Now with all this excellent advice on tap you should be making a great success of it. However, if you have a feeling a "Dear John" is on its way, here are the eight signs that she is going to end it

She hasn't called you for a few days.

Is she trying to pick fights with you?

She is being secretive

She no longer refers to "we" but "I".

She is spending more time with her friends.

You no longer talk much.

Friends start asking what is wrong.

She is very critical of you.

Now here's one for the ladies, the five male types you should avoid dating at all costs

FIVE MEN TO AVOID

Mother's Boy.   Probably lives with her and has a freezer full of homemade meals courtesy of her.

Tell him you don't like his mother to get rid of him as he will always side with her.

The Body Builder. Usually very vain, has photos of himself all around the house, loves himself more than anyone else and spends more time in the bathroom than you do. To get rid of him ask him to give up the gym for you

The Womaniser. Worse than a Sailor with a girl in every port. Treats you really well and tries to impress, but he does that with all the women. May have difficulty remembering your name and his mobile is always busy. To get rid of him tell him you used to be a man until you had the op last month.

The Workaholic. On a great career path but you have to make an appointment to see him and his work will always come first. Dresses smartly and eats in the best restaurants. Best way of getting rid is to say that you are taking a year off to travel and would he like to come.

Your Teacher/University Lecturer. He could be older, a little wiser and gives you a good grade. However, if your friends found out you could be accused of sleeping your way to success and he could lose his job. Best way of getting rid is to say someone is blackmailing you and if you don't stop seeing him, it will be reported.

In addition, do be careful of the following:

Anyone who plays golf

Any man who likes ceroc dancing

Any man who asks for a picture of you with no clothes on.

(unless he offers you money)

Any man with more than one James Blunt album

Train spotters

Bird watchers

And here is another one for the ladies:

THE TEN MOST DANGEROUS MISTAKES YOU CAN MAKE WITH MEN

Betting your life and love life on his "potential"- he may not wish to improve or change

Assuming you understand male psychology – men are very different to women.

Pretending to be something for a man – it will backfire on you

Sharing "how you feel" too early – men will panic as it is happening too quickly.

Misreading the signals – that men send out or not reading them at all.

Relying on your ability to judge character – men are not

easy to figure out.

Expecting a relationship to make you happy – sometimes they do but not always.

Convincing him to love you – you will never change how a man feels

Appearing desperate – very difficult to hide but a turnoff

Not getting help and advice – use friends, books, internet or whatever.

If you want to find out what is going on and where, the best place is often the pub on a busy night. I decided to wander down the road and chat to various friends about their dating experiences over a few pints of "Dragon Slayer" best bitter. Here is what they said

Mike – I'm not a designer girl, she said getting into her BMW convertible clutching her Prada bag. The only reason she had a date with me was a free lunch and a bit of male shopping as a change from her usual retail therapy.

John – There's just too much choice these days, the process is flawed in so far as people are always looking for someone better than the one they have. In former days you had to choose from a much smaller pool in your immediate neighbourhood. Do women really have their heart in it as the amount of choice lessens the chance of connecting.

Tim – A woman who had been divorced three times told me that as a 45-year-old bachelor I stood little chance of attracting a woman. That was rich coming from a woman who had failed at marriage three times; would that make her a better catch?

Paul – I made contact with an attractive blond and arranged to meet her, she looked really good on her photo. I arrived at the pub and there was no sign of her. After about an hour I was just about to leave when there was a tap on my shoulder and a soft voice whispered my name. I turned around and nearly fell off the bar stool. My date was a very large dark haired hairy armed woman with a fine moustache. After I had recovered from the shock I bought her a drink and asked her why her profile photograph was so different from reality. She explained that she wasn't having much luck as she was so she thought a photo of someone else might help!

Finally, here is my woman test which you may find useful.

THE WOMAN TEST

CALL HER AND SAY YOU ARE ILL

1. She understands and hopes you feel better soon; in the meantime, can she do anything to help.
2. She understands but doesn't want to catch anything so suggests you call when better.
3. She is not very friendly and thinks it's an excuse.

CANCEL A DATE AT SHORT NOTICE FOR SOME UNSPECIFIED FAMILY REASON

1. She understands.
2. She is not very pleased.
3. She is really pissed off.

GO TO DINNER AND FORGET YOUR WALLET

1. She pays with a smile
2. She pays grudgingly
3. She pays but seems to think it's expensive

FALL ILL WHILE ON A DATE

1. She gets you home, asks if you want the doctor and tucks you up in bed
2. She gets you to your car and says she hopes you will be ok
3. She looks none too pleased and says she was looking forward to the desert

MENTION ANOTHER WOMAN IN PASSING

1. She asks if she was an old flame
2. She bristles and asks if you are still going out with her
3. She looks very jealous and asks you if you are hiding something

FORGET TO CALL HER DUE TO WORK
PRESSURES

1.   She understands and knows you have to earn a living
2.   She feels you are putting work before her
3.   She asks you to choose between work and herself

YOU HAVE AN UNEXPECTED LARGE BILL TO PAY AND CAN'T AFFORD A WEEKEND AWAY WITH HER

1.   She says she loves you, not your wallet
2.   She says why not put it all on your credit card
3.   She is completely hacked off because she was looking
      forward to it

These simple tests and others of a similar nature can tell you a lot about a woman through good times and bad and how she will react to a problem in your life. A girl who scores all ones is a little gem and worth holding onto.

WHAT YOU SHOULD DO NEXT - HOW TO MAKE A START IN THE DATING GAME

The very first thing I would suggest is to peruse a few web sites to get the general idea of how things work. A lot of the sites contain hints and tips to help you make a successful start and I hope this final chapter will enable you to prepare for and enjoy your first dates.

Some websites suggest that women use their real first names whereas others suggest a "pen" name specifically for the web site which can be changed from time to time. Their choice of name could help you in choosing your first victims.

For instance, if you are in to the larger ladies you could choose CADBURY GIRL from Hull or MAPLE SYRUP from Tadcaster.

If you are into feisty ladies and enjoy the challenge then how about FIREHORSE from Faversham, LYNNSPITFIRE from London, GRIZZLY BEAR from Dudley or BETTY RUBBLE from Accrington.

If you like your ladies with large melons then look no

further than BIG TOP 40 from Goole, BOOPY DOOP from Aylesbury, BUSTYLOVA from Sidcup or possibly BABYCAKES from Theydon Bois, just for a change.

If you are really keen on joining the site for plenty of the old rumpy pumpy then you may be inclined to select RED HOT JUJU from Poole, LITTLE TRIKE from Birmingham, KINKY TRACE from Consett, HOTPANTS from Halifax or LUSCIOUS LIZZIE from Liverpool.

Those seriously into oral sex would go for MUFTI from Mirfield, CHICKEN LEGS from Coventry, BLUE RUBY from Barnsley or GOLDEN SILK from Glossop.

In case there are male readers wishing to explore their feminine side I would recommend, TINKLEBELL from Tranent, PAMPERPUSS from Portsmouth and SPARKLEBACK from Shrewsbury.

Heavy drinkers could relate to HELEN VODKA from Exeter or SPRITZER 22 from Southampton.

Finally, for those that want the really weird and unusual how about:

INVISIBLE LIGHT

CUDDLY COD

KINGFISHERCRAPCLAIRE

SAGA BABE

MOLLYMOO

CLUMSY

VINGT TROIS

WILLOW BUNNY

HOW TO CREATE YOUR PERFECT PROFILE?

There are really just two elements, a good profile and, don't be shy, always post a photo.

PHOTOGRAPHS

Spend a bit of time on producing a really good set of photos showing you in reasonable close up, smiling and with nice eyes. Ensure you are fully clothed, smartly dressed even if casual and preferably doing something interesting but not with a pint of beer and a fag in your hand. If you are really cute about this you could post a few photos showing a suit, smart casual and action man signalling you are a man who is adventurous and can conduct himself well in any social situation. If you have any tattoos cover them up and I would recommend you remove any piercings unless you are looking for a Hells Angel, a Goth or a lady into alternative sexual practices.

You will get a much better response with a photograph, particularly if you disguise your hump. For a real killer shot wear a uniform or dinner suit for one of your photographs, it does something to a woman, but if you are a traffic warden, forget it.

If you are to really understand the dating game you also need to develop the ability to interrogate women's photos and get some idea of what the person might be behind them.

Let me give you some guidelines:

A very posed picture

Could be insecure, scary and delusional.

Bubbly and curvaceous

Porky but cheerful

Backpacker photo

Posh background, big teeth, enthusiastic and doesn't wash

Bedroom shot

Could be on the game.

With gay friend

Pretty, insecure, drinks too much and nervous with men.

Good cleavage

> Husband with secretary, high rent and guzzles chardonnay.

With Horse

> Strong gripping thighs.

Wearing sunglasses

> Airhead

With dog

> Check for disability.

Guitar playing

> Sensitive dope smoker.

Shaved head

> Plays for both teams, often at the same time.

A TERRIFIC PROFILE

Just follow these rules and you will be so pleased you may even remember me in your will!

1. HONESTY AND REALISM

Make sure that you are honest and accurate in the description of yourself and that your photo is recent. Don't misquote height and weight or create a fantasy around yourself that you cannot deliver. Check all your information is correct, if you have had no replies it may be that you have mistakenly entered your height at 2ft 6 inches!

2.   BE UPBEAT AND POSITIVE

Make sure you sound like someone interesting and fun to know. Don't introduce a single moan or suggestion of negativity; everyone wants to be associated with someone who appears to be a winner. Replace all negative statements with positive ones, eliminate any dislikes.

3.   BE EXCITING AND REVEALING

Tell everyone what really turns you on, but not sexually. State the matters that are really important to you, your soul mate could click with you immediately on reading your profile.

4.   BE KIND AND MAKE THEM LAUGH

Make your profile friendly and accessible, it will generate interest and may just catch the eye of your soul mate. You don't have to be a comedian but try to remember funny stories or experiences so you can make her laugh in your first few vital messages. Don't tell her everything at once, tease her a bit and keep her guessing, she will be intrigued to know more. Show that you are a warm person and hint that you enjoy romance within your humour.

5.   **EMPHASISE QUALITIES AND ORIGINALITY**

Don't boast about what you have but explain your human qualities, your kind heart and romantic nature. Your ability to listen and understand.

Be an individual, if you have unusual hobbies and interests mention them, don't follow the herd with walks, theatre etc.

6.   **FILTER OUT THOSE THAT YOU DON'T WANT**

You need to focus in on the kind of woman you really want by using your profile and a series of filters. For instance, you may wish to use height, age, interests, religion and all kinds of other filters to focus in on the woman you are really looking for.

Although not part of your profile it is worth considering at this stage the kind of gifts that women like and dislike which may be far removed from your male perception.

If you are looking at a first meeting, anniversary of some sort or her birthday, try one of the following, which should help you get your leg over

A handmade card, very personal, with comments on letting her know how much she means to you.

A single red rose, in its own pretty box.

A beautiful bunch of flowers, preferably delivered to her work place so all her mates can speculate upon what a romantic guy you are.

Small box of high quality personalised chocolates.

A candlelit dinner for two having previously bribed the wandering violinist to play her favourite tune by your table.

If you have a particularly good uniform wear it and pick her up early from work, carry her out of the office and whisk her away in your limo. Her mates will talk about it for weeks afterwards and be so jealous. Overtones of "An Officer and a Gentleman".

Take her off to the airport and fly her to somewhere romantic for the night, e.g. Venice, Florence, Amsterdam or Toulouse. I would not recommend Düsseldorf or Belfast.

Buy her silk lingerie but avoid the flannelette passion killers her mother used to wear. The lady shop assistants are always very helpful if you can explain, without being too explicit, what you are looking for, and don't forget it really brightens up their otherwise boring day. Whatever you do though, don't ask them to try it on so you can see what it looks like.

Give her your favourite photo of the two of you in a silver frame.

Give her a book of romantic poetry or even write one for her yourself.

Cook a romantic dinner for two at your place with all the trimmings so that she can admire your culinary skills. Make it good but not too good otherwise she may be worried that she cannot match your capabilities.

If you follow the above, I guarantee you will not go wrong but let's look now at the things that you should not buy for her or say on such occasions

A spare tyre for her car, even if she needs one she will not appreciate it for some reason

Cleaning equipment or cooking utensils

Electrical items, particularly those of a very personal nature.

Cheap perfume, it won't fool her.

Clothes, you will deny her the pleasure of shopping.

Gift voucher for weight watchers – you want to live, don't you?

Anti-wrinkle cream – ditto.

Get her a fiftieth birthday card when she is only forty-eight.

Get her a card about growing old, bus passes and drawing the pension.

Mention that she is getting more like her mother every day.

Say you have had to order a bigger cake to fit all the candles on.

Tell her she is just as beautiful as when she was young.

Assuming you have survived the above, I now want to consider ideas for that all important first date.

Most people would choose to meet for lunch, dinner or a drink and there is absolutely nothing wrong with that providing you are both chatty and there are no awkward silences in your conversation. If the lady, you are meeting is known to be a little quiet and shy you may wish to consider alternatives.

If you do decide to meet for a meal do ensure that your table manners and knowledge of the menu are up to scratch before the date. Also check out the prices, you don't want to stumble into a Michelin 5 star where dinner will cost you a week's pay. At the other end of the spectrum don't even think about Macs or Burger King. Fish and chips are ok in the right setting, not next to some dingy factory in darkest Bradford but while walking around a pretty harbour such as Scarborough.

If you have inherited the clumsy gene from one of your parents and are prone to waiving your hands around, knocking over glasses, dropping cutlery and tripping over tablecloths you may wish to consider one of my alternative activities set out below -

Cinema, let her choose the film but make sure you choose the seating. Preferably a double seat at the back so that you can get to know her better, particularly if the film is not to your taste.

The Beach, if the weather is good take a picnic, bottle of wine and find a nice secluded spot. Do your research beforehand so that you don't stumble on to a naturist or gay beach as this may not impress on the first date.

Picnic by the river, with wine and bread for the ducks, shows you are at one with nature. Avoid areas with playgrounds and cross river Tarzan swings.

Theme park, preferably outside school holidays and if she seems a lively lass. Make sure you don't consume large amounts of alcohol and a vindaloo the night before.

Ice Skating or roller blading, make sure you get some practice first so that she will have to lean on you. Check beforehand that she is not a past British champion or you will look a total twat.

Kite Flying, get one in the shape of a big dragon and practice beforehand. Let her hold the strings while you supervise from behind. Don't knock it if you haven't tried it!

A visit to the Zoo, everyone like animals, particularly baby ones. It could rekindle dormant maternal desires which will do you no harm at all later in the day.

A stately home, providing she likes that kind of thing. Most people do, even born again bikies have been known to enjoy.

Concert, her favourite band and have her dancing in the aisles.

Horse riding for beginners, great fun if she hasn't tried before.

A boat trip, at sea or on a river to admire the scenery. On some you can even enjoy a meal.

A steam train ride, through beautiful countryside. Just make sure you don't sit next to any anoraks or train spotters.

Go karting, but make it fun and non-competitive.

Visit caves or some underground complex, she may not have experienced this.

Take her snorkelling, warm weather essential but opens up a whole new world.

Believe it or not there are some distinct advantages for women once they are over fifty. Families have mostly grown up, they often have a greater clarity in what they want out of the rest of their lives and the sort of person, if any, they wish to share it with. Women will have a little more time to think about romance and fulfilment.

There is no reason why, at this time in life, it should not be exciting and enjoyable and absolutely no reason at all why women should not feel sexy.

Just think about it, no more periods, no fear of unwanted pregnancies with months of swollen ankles and twenty years of nappies, chicken pox, acne and debt to worry about. Just pop into bed with your chosen one and have fun while not worrying about pills, your calendar or inserting a diaphragm (ouch). OK your figure may be a little rounder but try to think of it as voluptuous and Rubenesque as no doubt he will. Above all be adventurous in bed, you may wish to try something that you have never done before and there is absolutely nothing wrong with that. If you like it you have added to your repertoire, if you don't nobody will force you to do it again.

At fifty your self-confidence and ability to handle almost any situation life can throw at you should be considerably greater than in your twenties. You will now have a better idea of your likes and dislikes and should be a better lover and know what turns you on and not be afraid to ask for it. You may now be much more adventurous in your choice of holidays and in the bedroom. If you are not, then do something about it, you only live once.

Of course dating after a long marriage comes to an end means that both men and women are out of practice and perhaps not as confident as they should be.

In the words of the astronauts you will therefore need to develop your own re- entry strategy, if you pardon the expression.

Dating after divorce is a bit like learning to ride a bike again, whoops, perhaps not the best expression. Some people would have been good at it and are now just a little rusty while others may not have been very good to start with and are now faced with doing something they may not have wanted to do in the first place.

It can be a nerve wracking experience and lead to a lot of anxiety. We are much more set in our ways than in our twenties plus everyone carries much more baggage of the emotional, personal and family variety than they did when they were younger.

Here are my tips to make it easier for you –

PROFILES

You need to focus your profile on the kind of person you really want to meet and not try to please everybody or be all things to all. Describe yourself accurately, how you see yourself as a person and what you have learned through your life.

PHOTO

Spend time on it and get it right.

MAKE CONTACT

Take your time but when ready send off a few messages to people you like the look of and await responses. It will get easier as time goes on and your selection skills will improve.

LIVE IN THE PRESENT

Don't dwell on the past too much, particularly your ex or failed relationships. Take care not to be negative or bitter, it will do you good not to be.

BE POSITIVE AND OPTIMISTIC

You have to move on and learn to trust and live again despite the pain of lost love and failed past relationships. Don't close your heart to love or no one will want to know you better. Give your heart slowly but gaining love is so thrilling it is worth the journey. It may take time to meet the right person but then you may be ready to give and accept love.

OK SO I HAVE STARTED –
WHAT DO I DO NOW

Good, now you are up and running with an excellent photo and profile, you have expressed interest in a few people and they you and you have just started meeting your first dates. Here is what you should do

DATE SLOWLY

Easier said than done but you have to learn not to rush things despite your initial feelings. Don't become possessive too early in a relationship as it could make men in particular run a mile. Remember you have no right to claim loyalty and fidelity until you are in a full sexual and emotional relationship so the other party is free to meet others until that time.

You may be keen to enter into a full physical relationship but this may be premature in terms of the emotional relationship. This in turn could lead to a short term liaison which is far from satisfactory.

Remember an unhappy relationship is worse than no relationship at all, if you really want it to succeed, take it slow. Make sure you see how the other person lives day to day and manages stressful situations. Spend time together

in the real world not just snatched weekends of passion in a
Bognor Regis hotel.

MAKE SURE YOUR EXPECTATIONS ARE REALISTIC

All the media and advertising hype in today's world can
often lead to unrealistically high and overblown expectations
around romantic relationships.

Girls imagine the Cadbury Milk Tray ex SAS man
abseiling down a rope from a helicopter with a box of
chocolates for them. Or a dashing handsome man on a
white charger sweeping them up and carrying them off to
some perfect life.

Men imagine their wives can make a home, raise a family,
and bring in money while remaining pleasant, physically
attractive and energetic in bed.

Real life just ain't like that unfortunately, it can be hard
work, stressful and demanding.

DATE WITH A PURPOSE

If you are looking at a long term relationship you have to
realise that anyone with a serious personality flaw is a no no.
If it makes you unhappy now, you will feel much worse in a
long term relationship. Send a Dear John or Jane as the case
may be and get on with your life.

You are extremely unlikely to be able to change someone

who has real problems with drink, drugs, physical abuse or temper tantrums for instance and they could drag you down with them.

Let us imagine that you have now found someone a bit special and have been on several dates with them, how can you be sure that it's worth pursuing? Well the easy answer is to simply find out more about them. You already know the qualities that you are seeking and those that you are not and you have enhanced your listening skills. Ask them questions as part of your normal conversation along the following lines

FIND OUT MORE

Ask slightly leading questions which will help to reveal their views on a variety of topics and what makes them tick. Listen carefully and try to remember as much as possible to write down later.

Try not to make it like a formal interview as; above all, dating should be fun.

IMPROVE YOUR OBSERVATION

Do more listening than talking, ask follow up questions, find out what makes them happy and sad.

Observe manners and actions such as punctuality, attitude to the waitress and "judge their judgements".

USE YOUR INTUITION

This will play a large part in deciding whether you wish to see that person again, for instance do you feel comfortable with them and can you be yourself. You do not want to go through life having to live up to another person's expectations or preferences. If on the other hand you feel relaxed, at ease and comfortable with a kind of total acceptance then this could be the person for you.

This could now be the right time to revisit what you are looking for in a partner in order to check your requirements against the person you are becoming involved with

Intelligence – there are academic types and practical types and those in between. You may like an intellectual conversation but that person may not be able to change a light bulb. Most people tend to want someone at broadly the same level but those with high IQ's often have difficulties in socialising.

Personality – Ideally you want someone in harmony with yourself or you may compliment each other e.g. a strong minded person with someone easy-going. Look at your friends to see what sort of people they are as this may help you in selecting a partner.

Appearance – most people know what they want but make sure the requirements are your own and not some advertising ideal which doesn't exist in real life.

Ambition – Broadly similar ambition seems to work best.

Chemistry – Basically the physical urge that draws two people together. Some people Value chemistry above all, others are more logical and reasoned in approach.

Spirituality – Refers to faiths and believes but only loosely connected to religion. It is more internal faith i.e., do you seek answers to problems by praying to God or do you solve problems yourself by logic.

Character – Reflects t he very essence o f a p erson's being and reveals attributes such as honesty, courage and commitment. Your chosen person may have different attributes to yourself but he should have a strong character and see your views as important.

Creativity – If you are creative yourself you may not gel too well with someone who is analytical and logical. Similarly, a creative person can fall short in other areas such as practicality.

Parenting – It is vital that you agree about the mutual desire for children or otherwise. If you want them check out your loved one's potential in this area.

Authenticity – in order to share a relationship both partners must be themselves, if you act a part the relationship will almost certainly fail.

OK now your partner has passed all the tests above, so you think you are in love, but how do you know love is real? or is it just lust?

Will it last or just be a temporary phase in your life?

Here are my tests:

Communication

How well do you know each other?

Do you talk or is it all pillow talk?

If you are on the right track you can discuss anything openly

You can argue amicably and come to a good compromise.

You are open and honest with each other about your feelings

If you are on the wrong track you don't know much about your partner

You are frightened to ask in depth questions about them in case of rejection.

You do not openly and honestly discuss your feelings

with each other.

Mutual frustration builds up because you don't discuss.

You resent each other and neither is prepared to forgive.

Love

Positive signs include standing by each other in a crisis

Making sacrifices to make your partner happy

You are truthful, honest and don't keep secrets from each other.

You are emotionally, physically and mentally compatible.

You are friends as well as lovers.

If you are on the wrong track when the going gets tough, your partner gets going.

Your partner is untrustworthy and has a roving eye.

Your partner lies and only tells the truth when found out.

There is little physical affection, laughter or

communication between you.

Your partner has been frequently unfaithful.

Respect

Positive signs include you accept your partner's faults and imperfections.

You support and accept each other's individual interests and identity.

You find time to listen and understand your partner's opinion.

If you are on the wrong track you criticize each other in public.

Your partner wants to spend all their time with you and will not give

You space.

Your partner is constantly trying to "improve" you and be something that you are not.

You cannot forgive and forget each other's mistakes.

Love is such a wonderful thing, life seems so much better, everything looks good, you walk with a spring in your step and unfortunately it diminishes our ability to think and make rational decisions.

It can overwhelm us and cloud our judgement therefore you need to look at it rationally in the cold light of day.

It is vitally important that both partners are similar in the important ways described earlier, and then their common ground tends to bind them together.

You have to look at the ways your partner deals with others, most people are on their best behaviour while dating. But how does your partner treat their family and friends for instance, this will give you a good insight into their character.

In a partner what you see is what you get, don't try to change them.

Don't play games, be as you really are.

If you have an argument, make up quickly thereafter, discuss it, learn from it and don't let it fester.

Know what you want from your partner and what you are or not prepared to compromise on.

So, hopefully you are in love and you live happily ever after, end of story.

But what if your precious relationship falls apart and you are naturally very upset and devastated.

Your first reaction is to probably wonder what you did wrong and a self-analysis will do no harm but remember it takes two to tango.

Whatever you do don't lose your self-confidence and don't become bitter, negative and withdrawn. Remember there are other apples on the tree and its fun picking them.

So pick yourself up, dust yourself off, and start all over again, and this is how you do it

Love Yourself

Have good self-esteem, appreciate your good points.

Don't take revenge

it lowers your dignity and sense of worth, exit with style.

Escape

analyse your former partner's ways, you may just have had a lucky escape.

Healing

    give yourself time to heal and just remember the good times.

Improve your life

    go on the holiday you have always wanted, take up old hobbies.

Lessons

    analyse the situation, create learning points and absorb so you don't make the same mistakes again.

Appearance

    be optimistic, positive and look smart, your next conquest could be just around the corner.

I do hope that you have enjoyed my book and will find it useful in your future relationships and remember

HAVE FUN AND ENJOY

BE POSITIVE

BE REALISTIC

BE ROMANTIC

BE OPTIMISTIC

And the lady of your dreams could be just around the corner!!